BUTTERFLY
GRAVE

BUTTERFLY GRAVE

ANNe CAssiDy

BLOOMSBURY

LONDON NEW DELHI NEW YORK SYDNEY

Bloomsbury Publishing, London, New Delhi, New York and Sydney

First published in Great Britain in November 2013 by
Bloomsbury Publishing Plc
50 Bedford Square, London WC1B 3DP

A CIP catalogue record for this book is available from the British Library

ISBN 978 1 4088 1552 6

Typeset by Hewer Text UK Ltd, Edinburgh
Printed and bound in Great Britain by CPI Group (UK) Ltd,
Croydon CR0 4YY

1 3 5 7 9 10 8 6 4 2
www.bloomsbury.com

To Alice Morey and Josie Morey
My favourite teenagers

ONE

Rose Smith thought about murder a lot. On the bus, on the way home from a Christmas shopping trip she stared at the passengers sitting opposite her as image after image forced its way into her head. There was the girl floating face down on the waters of a silent lake, her hair fanning around her like seaweed. A boy lying on a railway bridge, a single stab wound letting the life haemorrhage out of him; days later his girlfriend dead on the path of a rose garden. The drowned man who had his hands tied behind his back, his body washed up against a pier while holidaymakers looked on.

It was not something she talked about to her grandmother, Anna. Nor did she mention these morbid preoccupations to her stepbrother, Joshua. She kept them to herself, tightly shut away in her head. She only brooded over them when she was on her own.

She hoped they were the last deaths.

She got off the bus and wove her way through the late afternoon crowds and headed back to Anna's house.

When she got to the corner of her street she was surprised to see Joshua waiting for her. He was wearing the grey tweed coat that he'd bought in Camden Market a few days before. It reached past his knees and made him look like someone out of an old film. His hair was cut shorter than normal and he had stubble and looked a bit distracted.

'I tried ringing you,' he said, walking with her. 'Your phone kept going to voicemail.'

'I must have turned it off.'

'Your gran said you'd be back about five so I thought I'd wait.'

'What's up?'

'My Uncle Stu has had an accident. He fell off a cliff while walking his dog.'

Rose stopped walking, shocked.

'He's all right, I think. Broken bones. Cracked ribs. A touch of hypothermia. Well, he's not *all right* of course . . .'

'How big a cliff?'

'Big enough. It's called Cullercoats and is somewhere we used to walk the dog. The policeman I spoke to said that my uncle just lay there all night. It seemed that he fell on to a ledge that had bushes and stuff so he was sheltered from the worst of the cold but he must have been there for hours, not being able to move.'

'That's horrible.'

'I know.'

'Didn't he have a phone?'

'Usually, yeah. It must have fallen with him and landed somewhere out of reach.'

'He's all right, though? He's not . . .'

'No, Rose. He's not going to die.'

'I didn't mean that. I didn't . . .'

'It means I'm going up to Newcastle tomorrow instead of on Christmas Eve.'

''Course!'

'Skeggsie's happy to go a few days early so we're packing tonight. It means I'll be away longer than I planned but . . .'

'You have to go. 'Course you do.'

'Why don't you come with us?'

They'd reached Rose's house. Rose knew that Anna would be inside beautifully dressed as ever and possibly listening to classical music.

'Me and you and Skeggs? Would we fit in the car?'

'Sure. It would be a squeeze but it would be OK. In any case, with Stu in hospital it would be good to have you there.'

'Anna is expecting me to be with her over Christmas.'

'You can ask her. She can only say no.'

'I will. I'll ask her. I'll call you later.'

Joshua smiled and hooked his arm around her neck and gave her a kiss on the side of her face. Then he went off up the road. Rose's fingers touched her skin where the kiss had been. She stared after him, the familiar feeling of longing stirring in her chest. It was so good to see him, to be with him, if only for a few moments. She took a deep breath and got her front door key out of her pocket and walked into the house.

She put the shopping bags in her rooms and went downstairs. Anna was in her drawing room, sitting at the small antique desk writing in a notebook. There was music playing at a low volume. Rose decided she had to come straight out and ask about Christmas. She knew that Anna had made plans for both of them to visit some of her friends and for trips to music concerts at the Barbican and the Royal Festival Hall. She also said that she'd like Rose to accompany her to church on Christmas Day.

None of these things appealed to Rose but she'd kept telling herself that it would only be for a couple of days – the real Christmas holiday would be the time she spent with Joshua.

'Anna, I've just had some bad news.'

'Really?'

'Joshua's uncle has had an accident. He's fallen off a cliff and is in hospital.'

'A cliff? Goodness, that sounds dreadful. Is that why he came here earlier? I wondered. He looked a little upset. Is the poor man in hospital?'

'Yes and the thing is . . . Well, Joshua's going to Newcastle tomorrow to see him and I wondered . . .'

Say it, Rose, she thought. *Say it out loud.*

'If you didn't mind I thought I might go with him. Stay in his uncle's house. Try and help out a bit. I know it means leaving you alone . . .'

'Of course you must go, Rose.'

Anna stood up and closed the book she'd been writing in.

'It's just that he might need someone to . . .'

'I understand. It's good of you to offer. I'll be fine here. There are a number of events I turned down because I didn't want to bore you but I'll go to them now. I'll keep myself busy. You go off to Newcastle with Joshua. And of course give my good wishes to the poor man when you see him.'

Anna left the room. Rose frowned, puzzled, as she watched her go. Later on, after ringing Joshua to tell him the news, she could have sworn she heard her grand-mother singing quietly to herself as she went down the stairs. Rose hadn't been looking forward to spending Christmas with Anna. Was there any reason to suppose that Anna had felt differently? She sighed. Her grand-mother had changed a lot over the previous weeks. There was a time when Rose couldn't mention Joshua's name. Now Anna had accepted that he was part of Rose's life. Indeed she seemed relieved that Rose had someone else.

The next morning she lay in bed after her alarm went off. The rain peppered the glass and the wind slipped in and out of the trees making them shiver. She rubbed her eyelids. Even though the room was still dark she could see the outline of the clothes that she'd hung on the back of her door. A black jacket. Black trousers. Grey blouse. On the carpet were her black boots and her bag and rucksack. She was really going to Newcastle.

The clock showed 6.18. Joshua and his flatmate Skeggsie were coming for her at seven. Just before going to sleep she'd got a text from Joshua to say that his uncle was having an operation today on his leg. Other than that he was *comfortable*.

This certainly wasn't the Christmas they had planned.

Joshua and Skeggsie's term at Queen Mary College had finished the previous Friday. Rose's college had broken up for the Christmas holidays on the same day. Skeggsie, Joshua's flatmate, had intended to take Joshua up to Newcastle on Christmas Eve; Joshua to his Uncle Stuart's and Skeggsie to his father's house nearby. Skeggsie was actually excited about the trip. He'd told Joshua that he wanted to go and see the Angel of the North. He'd had an idea for an art project linked to it, involving photography and animation. He had a new camera that he wanted to try out and had asked Joshua to help him.

Joshua and Rose had shopped for gifts at Camden Market and Rose had bought an old crystal vase for Anna from an antique shop. Joshua had bought a second-hand leather bomber jacket for his uncle and a blanket with paw marks on it for his uncle's dog, Poppy. Skeggsie hadn't gone with them. He'd ordered his Christmas gifts online and they were sitting in plain brown cardboard boxes under his computers.

Now things had taken a different turn and Rose's elation about going with Joshua to Newcastle was tinged with guilt. She had to keep reminding herself that Joshua's uncle had had a bad fall. She was going to *help*, not to enjoy herself.

She carried her rucksack and bag down to the hallway. She placed them by the front door. She went into the kitchen to give her grandmother her Christmas present. She'd wrapped the vase in silver tissue paper and ribbon.

Anna was sitting at the table eating a croissant. Beside her plate was a miniature jar of jam. There were dozens of them in the cupboard. Anna liked a fresh jar every time. It was one of the things that sometimes made Anna's home seem a bit like a hotel.

'You all ready?'

Rose nodded. She placed the wrapped vase on the table.

'Here's your Christmas present. As I'm not going to be here.'

'How lovely! And here's yours.'

Anna held out an oblong package. Rose smiled but took the package without enthusiasm. Anna bought all her presents from two or three West End stores and she had everything wrapped in-house. The wrapping was like a small work of art, its corners at right angles, evenly tied with a ringlet of ribbon springing from the centre.

'Open it whenever you like. I thought you might like it.'

'Thanks,' Rose said. 'I'll take it with me.'

The doorbell rang.

'That's them.'

'You will tell Joshua how sorry I was to hear about his uncle's accident.'

'I will.'

The doorbell rang again.

'I should be off.'

She bent down to her grandmother who paused from buttering her croissant and offered her cheek for a kiss. Then Rose dashed along the hallway and picked up her bags. The Mini was a few parking places along the street. Joshua took her luggage and put it in the back of the car beside the stuff that was already tightly packed there.

'You all right?' she said, looking up at him.

He nodded. He held the door open so that she could climb in the back. They drove up the street and turned out of the main road into slow moving traffic. After a few moments Joshua half turned in his seat.

'I called the policeman dealing with Stu's accident late last night,' he said. 'Stu's not talking much. He's had painkillers but it seems that he also has a head injury.

'Maybe that explains why he didn't ring anyone.'

'No, that's not why he didn't make a call. They found his mobile on the cliff path. As though he dropped it while walking. They also found an empty half bottle of Scotch in his car.'

Rose didn't know what to say. She caught Skeggsie's eye in the rear-view mirror. He'd probably already heard this.

'So I'm not clear in my head now what happened. I've been thinking that he lost Poppy and went after her and fell over the cliff. On weekdays he normally took her to the local recreation ground but for some reason he went up to the cliff path. That's odd because it's a drive to get there and it's pitch dark and pretty dangerous. It's the sort of walk we did at weekends or summer nights, not in December. Now it looks like he might have been drunk and lost his way.'

'Perhaps he'd had a bad day in school.'

'Maybe.'

Joshua's voice had a tinge of anger to it.

'We'll probably find out more when we get up there,' she said.

Joshua turned back to the front. Skeggsie put the radio on. It was a talk show and they drove along quietly listening to it. After a short while Joshua started to fidget and Rose saw him struggling to get something out of his pocket. It was a small notebook and pen. He flipped the pages over a couple of times.

'Can we pull over soon?' he said. 'There's a black Mercedes that's been behind us ever since we left Rose's road.'

Rose felt her neck tense.

'I want to see if it's following us.'

'Sure,' Skeggsie said. 'Let's get through the next lights then I'll park.'

Rose turned round and saw a black car behind them. The driver was a grey-haired man and next to him was a woman of the same age. She frowned. They looked like a married couple. Why on earth would they be following the Mini?

She heard the indicator going and saw Skeggsie move out of the traffic and into an empty parking space. The Mercedes went past and Rose saw to her dismay that Joshua was writing down the registration number in the notebook. He closed it and put it on the dashboard. Skeggsie started the car up again but Joshua put his hand out.

'Hang on, let's give it a few minutes. When we get going again we should keep an eye out, see if it turns up further along.'

As they drove off Rose tried to stretch her legs but the seat and the footwell was full up with Skeggsie's plain brown boxes. On top of them was a small brown suitcase, old-fashioned and battered. It had hard edges so she couldn't lean against it.

She tutted silently and looked out of the window at the road, to the side and behind. The Mercedes was nowhere to be seen.

They were not being followed at all. It was just Joshua's anxiety.

TWO

A hundred miles later they were nearing the services. There was music playing in the car. It was a new band that Skeggsie had started playing since he'd hooked up with Eddie, a boy at university, who was on his course. It wasn't a sound that Rose particularly liked but still she was glad of it because she had been struggling to find things to talk about.

They had hot drinks and doughnuts in the services cafe and then Rose went to the toilet. Washing her hands, she dabbed some water on to her face to wake herself up. Then she stood back and looked in the mirror.

The glass was grainy and had smears across it. Her face was oval and her skin was pale. Her brown hair was jaw-length and she had a half fringe. Today she was wearing earrings, brilliant blue discs; the exact colour of the Blue Morpho butterfly that she had tattooed on her arm. They stood out against her black polo neck jumper. Joshua had bought the earrings for her as a Christmas present in Camden Market. *Put a bit of colour into your life, Rosie!*

he'd said giving them to her unwrapped and in advance of the festivities. They'd hung from her ears and seemed to move about in mid-air like flying creatures. He'd smiled when she put them on. Then he'd said, *You know what? You look just like Kathy.*

The comment had surprised her. Kathy, her mother, who had disappeared from her life five years before. She'd gone out for a meal with Joshua's father, Brendan, and neither of them had come back. They'd not seen them since.

Did she look like her mother?

She took a tiny pot of lipsalve from her coat pocket and smeared it across her lips and found herself looking at the mirror through a blur of tears. She pulled a tissue out of her pocket and dabbed at the corner of her eyes, not wanting to smear the make-up. Then she blew her nose and went outside.

Out at the car Skeggsie had his hand on Joshua's shoulder and Joshua was staring at his phone, looking pained. The traffic was thundering past, a torrent of noise.

'What's up?' she said.

'Josh's looking on the net at the local newspaper.'

'What's it say?'

'Read it,' Joshua said, pushing his mobile at her.

She looked at the small screen and saw a headline.

Mystery of Schoolteacher's Fall
Stuart Johnson, forty-five, a teacher at Kirbymoore

Academy had a fall on Cullercoats Cliffs on the evening of Wednesday 19 December. Police sources say that he lay on a ledge for over eight hours before he was spotted by a man walking his dog on Thursday morning. Friends of the teacher say that he was depressed after splitting up with his girlfriend and had taken to drinking heavily.

Rose scrolled down but there was no more, just adverts.

'I don't understand. Who are these *friends*? Who would say that? In any case I thought he and his girlfriend were all right,' said Rose.

'Maybe the police gave the story to the newspaper.'

'This is terrible. He's a teacher. This won't do his career any good.'

'Let's get going,' Skeggsie said. 'Sooner we get there, sooner you can talk to him. You know what that local rag is like – it'll print any old rubbish . . .'

Joshua nodded and put his mobile away. Skeggsie moved to the driver's door as Joshua pulled out his notepad and began to flick through the pages, looking at the nearby cars and vans.

'Just checking some car registrations.'

Rose stared at his bowed head, hoping he'd look up at her and smile, maybe even make a joke out of it. But he didn't. He continued thumbing the pages, looking cagily around at the lines of cars.

She caught Skeggsie's eye and gave a half shrug.

Joshua stared at both of them.

'We've got to be careful. Don't forget what happened when the Russian followed me a few weeks ago. I haven't forgotten it.'

Skeggsie nodded rapidly and got into the car. Rose followed.

She dozed on and off during the rest of the drive. From time to time she heard mumbled voices from the front of the car when Joshua and Skeggsie talked between music tracks. Then, just after Washington, they stopped for petrol. Joshua went to pay but Rose stayed in the car. She turned and extricated her small bag from the back and put it by her feet. She got out a wet wipe and patted it on her skin. She was feeling hemmed in by the car and fed up with the journey. She wanted to say, 'How long till we get there?' But that sort of comment was childlike. When the car finally moved off Joshua tuned in to a talk radio station. The presenter had a Newcastle accent and Rose wondered whether he was expecting to hear something about his uncle's accident. He had his arms crossed and seemed tense, staring straight ahead.

Rose worried about him.

In the last weeks, even without this recent drama, Joshua had begun to change. Instead of being confident he was now edgy and nervous. The easy-going attitude he had had when they first met up in September, after their five-year separation, had been chipped away by the things that had happened to them.

She remembered that first night. Then she'd been bursting with excitement about seeing him. She'd left her boarding school months before and become a student at a college in Camden. He'd started university in East London and although they'd been in touch for months via email they hadn't come face to face. Heading out to see him that night she'd been like some jittery girl on a first date. She'd seen photos of him but had no idea what it would be like to stand next to him, no longer a tall awkward boy who she had once lived with. Now he was flesh and blood, all grown up.

She hadn't been disappointed.

In the months since then a lot had happened, grim things alongside startling discoveries about what had happened to their parents. Throughout it all an odd thing had begun to happen to Rose. She developed a growing attraction towards Joshua. She had come to think of him as her stepbrother but in reality he was not related to her. Their parents were never married and there was no blood link between them. But the four of them had lived as a unit and Rose thought of him as the only family she had left in the world. And then when she finally met him some completely new and disturbing feelings began to grow. Every hug Joshua gave her, every time he touched her arm or grabbed her hand, she felt a powerful longing for him and wanted to kiss him. More than once she'd felt her lips drawn to his. She'd always stopped herself, though, pulled back, stepped away.

She had fallen in love with him.

She hid her feelings and tried to pretend that things were normal between them. Common law stepbrother and sister; that's what they were. It didn't explain the nights that she couldn't sleep or the thrill that went through her chest when he touched her hair or her neck or her fingers.

There had been times when she'd considered telling him. *I know we've always thought of ourselves as stepbrother and sister*, she might say, *but really there's nothing to stop us getting closer to each other*. And what if she had said it? She'd imagined the world stopping for a moment as he tried to work out what she meant. He might look at her with blank incomprehension. Or he might be shocked, angry even.

It might spoil everything.

After the shopping trip to Camden and the gift of the blue earrings, she'd given him the present she'd bought for him for Christmas: a book about world-famous bridges. He'd been pleased with it and began turning the pages immediately. Then he'd hugged her, the hug lasting longer than she'd expected. *I'll miss you*, he'd whispered, *when I'm up in Newcastle* and his hand had rubbed up and down her back and caused her spine to weaken and her skin to tingle. After what seemed like a long time he'd pulled away from her and looked, for a second, as if he wanted to say something.

That had been the time for her to speak. But she hadn't been able to say anything. Then the front door had slammed and Rose had stepped back, startled, aware that Anna had come home. The moment had gone.

Finally, after what seemed like hours, they were off the motorway and back on normal roads with traffic lights and pedestrian crossings. They were passing streets of houses, parades of shops, garages and warehouses. As they went on she saw more people walking along, some with pushchairs, dogs on leads, and shopping trolleys. There was noise as well: the beeping of car horns, the screeching of brakes and scraps of music coming from other cars.

The car had stopped in a queue.

'Tyne Tunnel,' Joshua said. 'We need to go under the river.'

They moved forward and in minutes were going underground, the car close to one in front, all heading in the same direction, a strange quiet descending, cut off from the noise and life out on the street. Then with a burst of daylight they emerged on the other side. Back on to suburban roads, heading towards Joshua's home. Rose opened her window slightly and noticed a tang of something in the air. She realised it was the smell of the sea.

Then the car turned into a street, slowed down and parked.

'Here we are,' Joshua said.

The houses were brick-built, semi-detached with front gardens. She was surprised. They reminded her of the house she and Joshua had lived in in East London, with her mum and Brendan, in Brewster Road.

'This is Newcastle?' she said.

'It's Whitley Bay. About twenty minutes from the city centre.'

They unpacked the car and Skeggsie went off to his own house. After he'd gone the bags sat in the hallway while Joshua opened the pile of letters that had built up.

Rose looked around.

The inside of the house was very similar to the one they'd lived in before. She walked along and peeked into the living room. There was a bay window just like the old house and a fireplace with decorative tiles down each side. Their tiles had had yellow flowers and she remembered the bottom one had been cracked. Here there were pink chrysanthemums, the tiles all intact. She walked further along the hallway. The door opened on to a big kitchen-diner, previously two rooms that had been knocked into one. It was all exactly the same as Brewster Road. Rose wondered if upstairs would have three bedrooms, one of them tiny and a bathroom at the back of the house.

Had Joshua ever noticed the similarities?

'Shall I make a hot drink?' she said.

Joshua nodded, distracted by the letters.

She went into the kitchen and filled up the kettle, found some cups in the cupboard and some coffee. While it was boiling she looked at the table in the middle of the room. It was dark shiny wood with matching chairs, each one neatly slotted into place. Their table in Brewster Road had not been so smart. It was wooden and square and had four odd chairs around it. One of its legs had been shorter than the others so that it was unsteady and seesaw-like.

As soon as Brendan and Joshua had moved in with her mother and her they'd become an instant family. The two of them had fitted neatly into the empty places at that kitchen table. They'd played games of cards and eaten meals there, sometimes at the same time. They'd cut up cakes and placed slices on porcelain plates. They'd read newspapers, opened letters and Christmas and birthday cards. They'd had arguments and made up at that table. Joshua had seen it as his job to fold up wads of paper and cardboard to fit under the dodgy leg so that the table was level. Then days later it was wonky again.

Joshua had been eleven, two years older than her. She'd been amazed by this tall, gangly boy who was sharing her house. He'd been at Big School and wore a posh uniform and did Latin and French. He'd called her Rosie, which she hadn't liked at first. His room had been tiny but still he filled it with computers and bits of old machines that he liked to fix. He fixed her computer whenever it wouldn't do what she wanted it to do. In return she would play him tunes on her violin. Occasionally she'd make him cups of lukewarm tea and cheese sandwiches with big spoonfuls of lumpy brown pickle which they sat and ate at the table in the kitchen.

'You all right, Rosie?'

Joshua's voice broke into her thoughts. He was standing at the door of the kitchen with the letters in his hand.

'Sure,' she said, turning back to the kettle and pouring boiling water into the cups.

'You have been careful lately?' Joshua said. 'No sign of anyone watching you? On the way to college? While you're there?'

'No,' she said.

She'd answered these questions a number of times in the past weeks. It wasn't just cars following them that Joshua worried about. It was people as well.

'You do look around and see who's there at college? And on the train? And out of the house window? Just to make sure no one is hanging around?'

'I do. Honestly, I do.'

She gave a wan smile.

'We can't let our guard down, Rosie. We have to be careful all the time. It's a dangerous world.'

His forehead was crinkled into lines. She wished he

could mend this like he mended her computer and the dodgy table.

But he couldn't. His uncle was in hospital and his dad and her mum were still missing. There was no easy fix.

THREE

The doorbell rang. Rose went to answer it.

A blonde woman stood there holding a dog. She wasn't wearing a coat and had car keys hanging from her free hand. Her hair was pulled back into a ponytail, the kind worn by a young girl.

'I'm Susie,' she said. 'I used to be Stu's girlfriend? I've brought Poppy back.'

Poppy strained on the lead. She had seen Joshua behind Rose in the hallway. Susie unhooked her and she raced towards him, jumping up on her hind legs. Rose stood back. The dog was white and brown and looked something like a collie. When she leapt up at her Rose patted her gingerly, turning away slightly to fend her off. She didn't like dogs much. Poppy's claws scraped on the floor and her panting and squeaks of delight filled up the hallway. Joshua squatted down and she lay on her back, her tail swishing across the boards.

'You're Joshua,' the woman said bluntly. 'Susie Tyler.

We finally meet. Have I come at a bad time? Well, I know it's a bad time . . .'

'No please, come in . . .'

'Poppy's missed you,' Susie said.

'I've missed her.'

There was an uneasy silence.

'Let's go in the living room,' Rose said, feeling awkward.

'Poppy can go in the kitchen till she calms down,' Joshua said.

He made little clicking noises and patted Poppy as she went backwards and forwards excitedly along the hallway. Rose walked ahead of Susie into the small living room at the front of the house.

'Cold in here,' Susie said. 'This room's always cold.'

Susie looked terrible, Rose thought. Her hairstyle was severe and her skin looked drained, yellowish. She had on jeans and a baggy jumper, the cuffs covering her hands. She sat on the sofa and crossed her legs, her elbows on her knees, a huge diamanté 'S' hanging from her car keys. Joshua came back into the room.

'You want a drink? Tea? Coffee?'

Susie shook her head. 'I'd have a smoke if I hadn't given them up two weeks last Tuesday. How is Stu? Have you seen him?'

'No. We've only just got here. I know he had an operation today.'

Joshua sat down.

'But he's going to be all right, though? There's no lasting damage?'

'I don't really know.'

'I'd like to see him but . . .'

'Susie, what happened with you and Stu? The newspaper said he'd broken up with you and was drinking heavily.'

'Right. So you weren't in touch with him at all? I mean he didn't tell you what had been going on between me and him?'

'He wasn't much of a talker.'

'I might as well come straight to the point. I'm married.'

'Oh.'

'Stu knew I was married. At least he knew I was still living with my husband but we weren't close. Living in separate parts of the house. The trouble is it's not black and white. You love someone. You don't love someone. You get married, you fall out of love, you get a divorce. Simple. But love's not like that . . .'

'Susie, I just want to know about Stu?' Joshua said gently.

'Right,' she said, sniffing, sitting up straight, using one hand to pull the oversize jumper further down her legs. 'I met Stu at a vintage car rally. My sister's husband is mad for old cars so we went. My sister recognised Stu because he taught my nephew History. Anyway I went to get a couple of teas and Stu was there and we started talking. He told me about the classic MG Roadster he had in his garage, said he was bringing it back to life. Asked me if I'd like to come and look at it and I asked if he tried that line with every woman he met. Anyhow I work at Morrisons, in the pharmacy. And I saw him there a couple of days later and he asked me round to his house for a meal and that's how it all started. At the time me and my husband Greg were talking about splitting up. We'd never been able to have children, see. We'd been through counselling and stuff but we were just about done.'

'Did Stu know? Right from the beginning?'

'He did. I told him that me and Greg hadn't slept in the same bedroom for two years.'

Joshua glanced at Rose and then looked down at the carpet. He didn't speak. The only sounds were Poppy's tiny moans coming from the kitchen. Susie didn't seem to notice his embarrassment.

'And we had made an appointment to see a solicitor but when it came to it we never bothered. Then I met Stu and I told Greg I was leaving but Greg broke down and . . . I couldn't . . . See Greg is a partner in a cafe just off the Promenade? The Blue Kettle. His partner's ill and the bills are coming in. The business might go bust. And we've been together for fifteen years. On top of everything I suppose me leaving him was too much.'

Susie took a deep breath.

'So I finished it with Stu. He kept contacting me, though. Phoning me, hanging round Morrisons. Greg saw him there last Friday and the two of them had a fight. Stu hit Greg and knocked him out. That was the last . . . the last time I spoke to him.'

Susie's eyes glassed over. Rose watched as a tear slid out of the side and ran down her cheek, leaving a trail on her skin. Susie pulled out a white cotton hanky from her back pocket. It had been folded up and ironed. As she shook it out its creases stayed. She blew her nose and then bunched it up in her hand.

'I heard about his accident from my neighbour whose husband works in the police station. I couldn't believe it. I went straight there and arranged to get Poppy.'

Susie stood up.

'So it's all finished between you and Stu?'

She nodded. 'I'm back with my husband. We're giving it another try. Look, I should go.'

Her fingers were up to her lips as though there was a cigarette there. Then she walked out into the hallway.

'Thanks for looking after Poppy.'

'I'm sorry for what happened, Joshua. I mean, about me and Stu and Greg. I never set out to make a mess of things but it just got out of hand.'

Joshua opened the front door.

'I feel bad saying this but I won't be visiting Stu in the hospital. Greg wouldn't like it. Will you tell your uncle when you see him? I do care about him but it's better for me and Greg if . . .'

Then she was gone. Joshua closed the door.

He seemed stuck to the spot.

'So that's why Stu was drinking heavily. She chose her husband over him. It's such a cliché. He had a broken heart. He drank too much and lost his way on the cliff. Nothing but a stupid accident.'

Later Rose unpacked her stuff in the box room at the front of the house. It was tiny and had a window overlooking the street. The bed had no sheets on it, just a duvet spread across the mattress and a pillow. There was a chest of drawers and some hooks on the back door. Three wooden hangers hung from them. It felt as though it was a room that no one had ever slept in or used.

She walked across to the window and looked out into the street. It seemed fuller now than when they first drove up, cars and vans parked along each side, one van further along double-parked. Most probably delivering something, Christmas presents perhaps.

She could hear Joshua downstairs. The television was on and he was channel-hopping. She walked out into the hallway and put her hand on the banister rail. The layout of rooms on this floor was the same as their old house. The same tiny box room had been Joshua's and hers was across the way where Joshua's bedroom now was. Her mum and Brendan's bedroom had been at the back next to the bathroom. It overlooked the long and overgrown garden that no one ever seemed to have time to sort out.

How happy they had been.

Until the day they lost it all.

On 4th November her mother and Brendan went out for a meal and Rose and Josh had a babysitter. Rose was allowed to stay up until they got home. She sat with the baby-sitter, Sandy, watching television and chatting.

The air was pungent with the smell of fireworks, the sounds popping all evening. Sandy started to get worried about eleven and her dad came round. He told Rose everything would be all right and that she should go to bed so she did. Joshua hung about on the landing. Rose saw him there early the next morning. He was still wear-ing the same clothes. He hadn't gone to bed at all. *Are they back?* she'd asked, fearful because somehow, deep inside, she knew they weren't. The house gave it away. Her room seemed bigger, emptier. The central heating seemed to moan as it came on and the windows rattled as though something was locked outside. *Are they back?* she'd said.

Without turning round Joshua shook his head.

Kathy and Brendan were gone and no one knew where or why.

A policeman came to see them later. He sat with them at the kitchen table. He made them drinks. Joshua's tea was too hot and hers too sugary. They looked at each other in a bewildered way when he told them their parents were missing and that they'd have to spend a short time in foster care until it became clear what had happened. Rose played with the place mat in front of her, straightening it up, turning it round. Then she got up and went upstairs to pack a bag.

A while later she met her grandmother for the first time. A social worker took her to a house in Belsize Park, explaining on the way about the existence of this relative whom she had never met. Rose expected an older version of her mother but what she got was something quite different. Anna Christie was tall and dressed smartly like someone about to go to a wedding. Rose was to go and live with her. She would have her own study and bedroom and her grandmother would arrange for her to go to a boarding school. Joshua was to go and live with an uncle in Newcastle. On the day she went to live there the social worker carried her bags and she carried her violin case. They'd had to park a bit away and Rose had trailed along behind. If she couldn't stay with Joshua then it didn't matter where she was. The front door opened and her grandmother led her up to her rooms and left her there to get settled in. She sat on the bed with her not yet unpacked bags by her feet. Adrift, floating away from the life she had once had. At the same time she knew that Joshua was on the train to Newcastle.

Everyone she cared about had gone.

*　　*　　*

The sound of footsteps on the stairs stirred Rose from her thoughts. Joshua was coming up. She went back into the box room and continued unpacking. She glanced out of the window again. The van that had been double-parked was moving away. Behind it was a silver SUV, a woman sitting in the driving seat. She peered at it. It was too far away to see the woman's features but the sight of the car made her feel anxious. There were thousands of silver SUVs around but weeks before she and Joshua had been hurt and threatened by a man driving one. She stared at it for a few moments before going back to unpacking. The door opened.

'You all right?' Joshua said.

She nodded.

'What about you? Did Susie upset you?'

'No. But I feel a bit angry with myself. I should have come back for a visit. Then I might have known what was going on. I don't know why I didn't. I just got sucked into college and all the stuff about Dad and Kathy. It seems like I forgot about Stu. Four months. I could have come home for a weekend and I didn't.'

Rose didn't know what to say. Joshua was right but she didn't want to make him feel any worse. He *should* have come home to visit his uncle.

'What time did Skeggsie say to come?' he said.

'About sevenish?'

'I'm going to go to the hospital.'

'Do you want me to come?'

'No, I need to see what's happening. Have a talk with Stu if he's able.'

Rose listened to his footsteps as he went downstairs and out of the front door. She watched him walking along the street. Looking back she saw that the silver SUV was still sitting there. Looking harder she thought she could see a dog on the passenger seat next to the woman, its front legs up on the dashboard. At that moment the offside indicator blinked on and off and the car pulled away from the pavement and drove off. She felt instantly stupid. It was just someone stopping for a phone call or to look at a map or just to take a ten-minute break from driving.

A woman and her dog.

She mustn't get suspicious of everything. Not like Joshua.

FOUR

They had shepherd's pie at Skeggsie's house. Skeggsie's dad, Bob, carried it in from the kitchen with a flourish. He was a big man with a mop of silver hair. He was wearing blue jeans and a check shirt with a suede waistcoat over the top and looked, Rose thought, as though he was going to a barn dance. He was *nothing* like Skeggsie.

'Stu was still groggy after the operation,' Joshua said, answering Bob's question. 'They had to put pins in his knee so he's in a bit of pain. They're doing an MRI scan of his brain in a few days because they think there might have been a bleed. He's not in ICU so they don't think he's in danger but it's all pretty unsettling. Seeing him like that.'

'Awful. Does he remember what happened?'

'I didn't ask. He was drifting in and out of sleep so I came away. I'll go again tomorrow.'

'He looks bad now but he'll be up and about soon. Probably not in time for Christmas.'

Joshua shook his head and they ate their meal. Rose looked around the room. There was a sideboard along one of the walls. The top was covered in photographs of a woman and a child, probably Skeggsie. The others showed the woman next to Bob, in his police uniform, both of them smiling brightly into the camera.

After eating Bob carried the dishes into the kitchen. Skeggsie spoke in a loud whisper.

'Do you mind if we get out? Make some excuse. There's some stuff we need to talk about.'

Bob came back into the room, smiling.

'Can we help you wash up?' Joshua said.

'Not at all, lad, you sit down.'

'Actually, Dad, we thought we might go to the Lighthouse for a drink.'

'You're welcome to join us?' Joshua said, ignoring Skeggsie's shocked look.

'No, no. Music not to my taste there. No, you kids go off. You'll have your key, Darren, so I won't wait up for you?'

'Yep,' Skeggsie said.

He strode out into the hallway and put his coat on. Rose was slightly embarrassed by his haste. She smiled at Bob and followed.

'You'll eat here on Christmas Day? I absolutely insist,' Bob said.

'That'd be good, thank you,' Joshua said.

Then the three of them were outside the front door, doing up their coats. Without a word Skeggsie strode off and they followed him.

They headed towards the seafront and within minutes were walking along the Promenade. On one side of them were the lights of the town, some garish Christmas decorations and others that looked as though they were left over from the summer illuminations. On the other side was thick blackness, the sound of water slurping heavily from side to side. There was no wind but it was bitterly cold. Rose tucked her hands up into her sleeves and pulled the edges of her hood closer to her face.

The Lighthouse was halfway along the Promenade. It was old-fashioned and a little tatty. Inside it was hot and dark. There was music on and a few people dotted around.

'We used to come here all the time,' Joshua said, raising his voice.

'We'll sit in the back. It's quieter there,' Skeggsie said.

Rose followed Joshua as Skeggsie went to the bar to get drinks. They headed through some doors to another room that was well lit. It had a high ceiling and sofas and low tables. The walls were covered with old photographs of fishermen. They sat in a corner far away from the main bar. Across the way a couple of men were playing darts. One of them was young, wearing a suit but no tie. The other was older, in baggy jeans with big turn-ups over heavy duty boots. They looked like father and son.

'I think Skeggs wants to talk about the notebooks,' Joshua said.

Rose didn't answer. *The Notebooks*. It was a kind of shorthand for talking about the search for their missing parents, something that Joshua was passionate about. The police had always had their own version of events. Kathy and Brendan, both police officers, working on cold cases, had been killed because of an investigation they were involved in. Their disappearance and death was *in all certainty* at the hands of organised crime. They had, *no doubt*, come close to uncovering the guilt of someone in a high place and it had cost them their lives.

But Rose and Joshua now knew that the police had not always told the truth. They, with the help of Skeggsie, had established that their parents were *not* dead. All they had to do now was to actually *find* them. The last firm sighting of them had been eight months before in Cromer.

But Stuart's accident had put everything on hold.

Skeggsie was walking towards them with the drinks. He placed a tray on the table. He handed a bottle of beer to each of them. Rose took hers and sipped it.

'*Thank you, Skeggsie*,' Skeggsie said under his breath, half joking.

'Thanks, mate,' Joshua said.

Rose mumbled, 'Thanks,' her mouth full of fizz.

'We ought to clarify where we are with the notebooks,' Skeggsie said.

'I can't really get my head around this right now . . .' Joshua said.

'I know that,' Skeggsie continued. 'But we need to be clear about some stuff. Since meeting James Munroe things are different. I just want to make sure we're all on the same page.'

James Munroe.

Rose remembered the ex-Chief Inspector from a few weeks before when he'd turned up at the flat in Camden with information for them. She'd first met him when she was a grieving twelve-year-old. He now no longer worked for the police force, he'd said, but was a civil servant and had information about where their dead parents' bodies were. There'd even been a memorial service for her mother, which James Munroe attended wearing a dark Crombie coat and looking suitably pained at the event.

But it had all been a lie. A fabrication.

'Skeggsie's right,' Joshua said, sighing. 'There are things we need to sort out.'

'OK, since meeting James Munroe everything has changed. Because of what he told us it has to *appear* that we're shutting down our search for Kathy and Brendan. It has to seem as though we believe his story.'

The darts game had finished and the older man was cheering his own victory. The young man was shaking his head as if he couldn't believe the result. 'Best of three?'

the older man said and the young man nodded in a resigned way.

'From now on we have to do things differently,' Skeggsie said, lowering his voice as though he suspected that someone was listening in on their conversation. 'So no email or text messages on each other's mobiles.'

Joshua grunted.

'We've closed our websites down. We don't discuss your parents in blogs, tweets, Facebook or any other place on the web. These things can be accessed by other people. The only way we three should connect up is by word of mouth or phone call.'

This meant that Rose could no longer use her personal blog Morpho.

'Then there's the physical stuff. I didn't want to leave it in the flat so I've brought it with us.'

'The physical stuff?' Rose said, confused.

'He means the butterfly book and Dad's things, his maps and all the stuff to do with the cottage, the Cromer photographs.'

Rose had a mental image of the old hardback book called *The Butterfly Project*. It looked as though it had sat on the shelf of some library for years before anyone had taken it out.

'And the notebooks,' Skeggsie said.

The two notebooks were the size of exercise books. Each held a photograph and pages of coded writing. Each book was concerned with a murder. Of all the things they had discovered these books had proved the most mysterious.

'All the stuff's in a suitcase in my room. My dad's house has very up-to-date alarms. When we get back to London we should invest in a safety deposit box. It may be months before we can decipher the notebooks and if they were to get stolen or anything . . .'

'You're right. We'll do that when we get back.'

'Just as long as we all know that that job still has to be done and until the notebooks are decoded we can never really be sure of what all this is about.'

'I get that. I totally do.'

There was quiet for a moment and it looked as though Skeggsie might have something more to say. Across the room the door opened and a young man and woman came in from the other bar. Snatches of music came with them. The young man called out.

'Darren!'

Skeggsie looked round. Joshua sat up stiffly, a frown on his face. Rose felt the tension rise and looked again at the young man. He was walking towards them with the girl. He was wearing a parka, his stomach sticking out at the front. His hair was cropped and he looked a little drunk. The girl was wearing drainpipe jeans and a tight V-neck jumper. Her hair was dark and hung down each side of her face. At the V of the jumper Rose could see the dusky line of her cleavage.

'All right, Rory?' Skeggsie said, tight-lipped.

'Darren, my old mate, you've come back to see us.'

'He's not your old mate, Rory,' Joshua said.

'Still got your bodyguard. No need now, though. That's all in the past. No need to be enemies any more.'

'Anyone want to say hello to me?' the girl said, her hands on her hips in a petulant way.

'Hi, Michelle,' Joshua said, looking down at his knee.

Another face appeared at the door. A young black man in a denim shirt. He was carrying a pint of beer and headed straight for them, smiling.

'All right, Skeggs? Don't take no notice of Rory. He's a teddy bear now. Well, he's as fat as a teddy bear,' he said, patting Rory's stomach.

'Martin,' Joshua said, relaxing, moving out from behind the table.

Martin put his glass down and then took up a boxer's position as if he were in the ring ready for the bell to go. Joshua smiled and gave him a playful slap on the head.

'What's going on? I heard about your uncle. Terrible!'

Rory was standing still. Michelle had threaded her arm through his and was saying something in his ear. Skeggsie hadn't moved an inch. They were looking straight at each other. Rose felt the animosity between them. Martin noticed it as well.

'Lighten up. We're all mates now. School days are gone.'

Rory nodded, a half-smile on his face.

'Come on!' Michelle said.

She pulled him by the arm so that he was walking across the room. In moments they were gone.

'Rory doesn't do that stuff no more. He goes to my boxing club. Trying to work off some weight. He's a changed man.'

'Yeah, right,' Joshua said.

Martin continued to talk to Joshua. Rose could hear Stuart's name being mentioned over and over again.

'You all right?' she said to Skeggsie.

'Yeah. I knew he'd be around but I wasn't expecting him to turn up just then.'

The two men who had been playing darts had finished.

'You want to play?' he said to her.

She shook her head.

'I'll play with you, mate,' Joshua said. 'Martin, meet Rose, my stepsister . . . sort of . . .'

'I thought she was your girlfriend!'

Rose managed a smile but felt her cheeks heating up with embarrassment. Skeggsie had gone off to the dartboard and Joshua had followed him. Martin was staring at her.

'You don't say much, do you?'

'When someone asks me something sensible I'll answer.'

Martin went to speak but stopped himself. He looked curious. He stepped across to the sofa and sat beside her where Joshua had been.

'You at uni?' he said.

'Sixth form.'

'Doing what?'

'English, Law, History . . .'

'I'm at York. Computer Science and Engineering. Me and Josh. We're going to build bridges.'

'That's all Josh ever talks about. Engineers must build other things.'

'Yeah, but think where society would be without bridges. Think about how long it would take to get from here to South Shields. Days! Did you know that there are twenty-two bridges across the Tyne?'

'Twenty-two!' Rose said, picking up her beer.

'You know you're quite nice-looking. Has anyone ever told you that? Maybe a little bit of make-up might improve . . .'

Rose spluttered in outrage into her drink.

'I'm not interested in what you think about how I look. I look the way I like to look.'

'Sorry. I speak without thinking.'

Rose huffed. Then she softened. It was something she did a lot. Saying things before thinking them through. She changed the subject.

'What was all that about with that boy, Rory?'

'Ah! Past history. Rory Spenser used to be a very bad boy. In school he had a way of relieving other people of their money. He'd go up to younger kids and say, *Don't you owe me some money?* And they'd say *How much?* And he'd say, *How much you got in your pocket?* And that way Rory built up a bit of a reputation. Now he's a changed man.'

'He did this with Skeggsie?'

'That and more. Although Skeggsie never did himself any favours in school.'

'That doesn't excuse people taking advantage of him.'

'I know. Rory was nasty. But believe me, he has changed.'

'What changed him?'

'He got beaten up a few times. He began to know what it felt like to be on the receiving end.'

'Who by?' Rose said, as Martin's eyes slid towards Joshua.

'A few of us. He's got an older brother and we had to explain it all to him as well. We saw it as a kind of community service. Now Rory's more careful what he does.'

Rose frowned. 'But doesn't that make you just as bad?'

'No, it stops the problem. I got no regrets about helping Rory improve his interpersonal skills.'

Rose felt there was something else to say but didn't know what. ˜

'But enough of this,' Martin said. 'How long are you up for?'

'Till New Year.'

'Great. I'll no doubt see you around with Josh.'

Martin stood up, went across to Joshua and said something, patting him on the back, before going back into the other bar. Not long after, Joshua and Skeggsie came back to the table, the game of darts over.

'Let's drink up and go,' Joshua said.

On the way out of the pub they passed Rory Spenser, who was on his own, standing by the bar holding a pint of beer. His eyes followed them all the way through. Rose looked round and saw Skeggsie staring down at the floor.

Outside the cold bit into them and Rose did her coat up and hugged herself. She looked into the darkness and felt the sea out there, huge and silent.

'I'm going home,' Skeggsie said, backing away. 'I'll be round in the morning about ten?'

'Sure.'

He walked off. Rose turned to go in the opposite direction but Joshua pulled at her sleeve.

'Wait a sec.'

A few moments later the pub door opened and Rory walked out, looking round, his eyes following Skeggsie as he walked up the Promenade and then turned down a side street.

'Where you off to?' Joshua called.

'What's it to you?'

'Leave Skeggsie alone, Rory. I've told you before . . .'

'Or what?'

Joshua looked at Rose and then seemed to hesitate. 'You know what. Just remember the last time.'

Joshua walked off and Rose followed. She glanced back and saw Rory in the same position as before, his face pale and round. She had to hurry to keep up with Joshua, who was walking swiftly, his shoulders rounded. A tinkle of laughter came from a nearby group of people as they turned off the front and headed towards the back streets and Stuart's house.

FIVE

The next morning Skeggsie drove them to the hospital. It was a twenty-minute drive and no one said much. When they parked outside Joshua sat for a moment, not opening the door.

'Do you guys mind if I go and see Stu on my own? I don't think he's ready for anyone who's not close family.'

'Are you sure?'

He pushed the handle and the passenger door opened.

'I'll make my own way home. Just expect me when you see me.'

'I'll come and pick you up,' Skeggsie said.

'No. I'll get the bus.'

'Right,' Skeggsie said.

'Maybe you two can spend a bit of quality time together,' Joshua said with a wan smile.

They watched as he walked towards the entrance of the hospital, his big coat flying out behind him. Then Skeggsie spoke.

'There's something I want you to look at. It's at my house.'

He drove off and Rose felt her spirits sink. This had to be something to do with the notebooks. The car shot along the dual carriageway and then turned off for Whitley Bay. She sat silently, holding in her irritation. After what Joshua said the previous evening about leaving it until they got back to London Skeggsie was still going on about it.

'I've decoded some more of the notebook,' he said. 'There are some puzzling bits and I'm not sure how to tell Josh. I mean I wouldn't tell him *now*, with all this going on, but I'll have to tell him sometime.'

'What is it?'

'I've had this decoding programme running on the text for days now. You remember I told you that the code changes every few lines? Like on one line A equals L? Then two lines down it changes and A equals P. It seems that the basic key is the same on each page. Paragraph, Line, Letter. So it's paragraph four, line three, letter two. The only thing is that every couple of lines the page number changes. So you get two lines of text then the code doesn't work any more. You have three hundred and forty-eight other pages of *The Butterfly Project* to choose from. Well, that's not strictly true because at least a hundred of the pages are covered in drawings and diagrams but it leaves approximately two hundred and forty-eight pages to go through until you start to get a word. So a couple of days ago . . .'

'Enough about the code, just tell me what it says.'

There was a moment's silence. Then Skeggsie spoke, his voice tight.

'I've printed off a page of it and I'll show it to you when we get back to my house.'

'Don't go all moody on me. I just can't get excited about a silly old code!'

Skeggsie put the radio on loud. It was a talk station. Rose would have preferred music but she let it go rather than ask him. The traffic was moving slowly.

Rose slipped into thinking about the notebooks.

Joshua had taken both books from the man who had given them the information that their parents were still alive. The first page of each was a photograph and there were some maps and diagrams and pages and pages of coded writing. It wasn't until they found a dog-eared copy of *The Butterfly Project* among Brendan's belongings that they thought they might have a way to break the code. Skeggsie had been working on one of the books ever since.

After crawling through traffic they finally reached Skeggsie's house. Rose waited while Skeggsie unlocked the Chubb lock then the Yale and then punched in a code for the burglar alarm before they went inside. She was reminded, for a second, of the way that Skeggsie used to lock the Camden flat door every time someone came in or went out. Lately he had not been so nervous about security.

'Come up to my room,' Skeggsie said.

Rose trudged up the stairs behind him. Once in his room she looked around and saw, without surprise, that it was arranged almost identically to the one he had in London. On one side was a neatly made bed. On the other was a big desk. Here the only computer he had was his laptop. On the wall behind it was a large picture of the Angel of the North. Rose's eyes were drawn to it. It looked like some computer-generated alien, its face featureless, its body striated with ridges. Its wings were vast, one giant slab of steel cutting through the soft rounded body.

'Ever seen it? Close up, I mean,' Skeggsie said.

She shook her head.

'Its wings are the width of those of a jumbo jet.'

'Really?'

'Josh and I were going to go but now I'm not sure . . .'

'There'll be time. Get Christmas out of the way.'

Looking down at the desk Rose saw the notebook that Skeggsie had been working on. She sat down on the chair and picked it up. She hadn't seen it for a while and she lifted the front cover to see the familiar photograph of Viktor Baranski, the former Russian navy man who had become a millionaire businessman. He had settled in London and was rumoured to have given secrets to the British government. It was also thought that he was involved in trafficking.

They knew that her mother and Brendan had been investigating Viktor Baranski and his organisation. They were looking into the discovery of five dead eastern European girls who were found in the back of a lorry. One of them was only fifteen. They built a case against him but then in 2006 he disappeared and turned up dead, in the North Sea. At the time it was said that he'd been killed by the Russian secret service as a reprisal for giving their secrets to the British. According to ex-Chief Inspector Munroe it was this very event that triggered their parents' disappearance. Baranski owed money to German gangsters and they blamed Brendan and her mum for not getting what they were owed.

Was any of it true? None of them knew for sure.

Rose flicked through the pages of code. On one was a diagram that she recognised. It showed a coastline and a village. It was Stiffkey in Norfolk, where their parents had stayed in a cottage. Weeks before Rose and Joshua had found the remains of an identity bracelet there that had belonged, they thought, to Viktor Baranski. It was also the place where Joshua and she had been roughed up and threatened by Lev Baranski, Viktor's son, the man in the silver SUV. Rose closed the book because she did not want to remember it. She saw that Skeggsie was holding a single sheet of A4 paper. He put it in her hand.

'This is the section I decoded. Read it.'

She took the piece of paper.

Operation VB

Viktor Baranski at an event in his restaurant,
Eastern Fare, 15th July at 17.30.

Afterwards will be making visits to other business
concerns, Property Ventures in Holborn and Elite
Buildings in Mayfair.

Approx. 20.30 he will then go to the flat of his
mistress off Oxford Street.

He is expected to be there for a couple of hours.

He is to be picked up after spending time with
this woman. He will have to be intercepted
inside building before his driver knows that
anything has happened. Important to use
restraints and gags.

Take care about SVR surveillance. Take note of
people, cars and cameras.

Once in custody Baranski should be passed on
to B.

Change cars.

B will take him to Stiffkey.

B will hand him over to F.

B will wait until operation is complete.

B will help dispose of evidence.

Rose felt uncomfortable. She read it over again and found
herself frowning. Viktor Baranski's body had been found
near Cromer, which was twenty or so miles from Stiffkey.

So this document, plan, whatever it was, had been written while Baranski was still alive. It was in fact a plan to *abduct* him.

'What's the SVR?' Rose said.

'The SVR is the Russian foreign intelligence service. Part of what used to be the KGB. Spies.'

'So you think that the Cold Case team kidnapped Baranski in order to hand him over to the Russian secret police?'

'Maybe.'

'But what about the case of the suffocated girls, the trafficking? Why was he not arrested for it?'

'Maybe they didn't have enough evidence for a trial. Possibly this was how they decided to resolve it. Hand Baranski back to his own people so that they could deal with him.'

'Perhaps they thought that Baranski would be taken back to Russia and put on trial.'

'I don't think so. That's why I'm a bit worried about showing this to Josh.'

Rose read over the document again. It didn't take long for Skeggsie's words to sink in.

'You think B stands for Brendan?'

Skeggsie nodded.

'And Brendan was the one who handed him over? At the cottage in Stiffkey?'

'It would make sense. That's where you found Baranski's identity chain.'

'But just because Brendan handed Baranski over that didn't mean he knew they were going to kill him.'

'It makes some sense of the threats Baranski's son made against Josh.'

Rose remembered Lev Baranski shouting at Joshua, *I have not forgotten my father's death and I never will.* It had happened at the cottage at Stiffkey.

'Look,' Skeggsie went on, 'it says *B will wait until operation is complete. B will help dispose of evidence.*'

Rose frowned. She read it over, studying each word.

'But that could mean literally clearing away any evidence that Baranski *had been in the cottage.* That's all. Handing the man over because of some deal done between the police and the secret services and then getting rid of any evidence. That's what it implies! What were you thinking?'

Rose's voice was getting louder. Skeggsie's was lower, calmer than before. It irritated her that he didn't get upset about anything.

'Could it mean that B had to dispose of the body?' he said.

'No! Don't be ridiculous. Of course not. You're reading too much into it. I think Baranski was probably handed over in good faith and that him turning up dead was the last thing anyone wanted.'

'Um . . .'

Skeggsie looked thoughtful.

'Look, we shouldn't mention this at all. Not until we get back to London. Agreed?'

Skeggsie nodded.

'I'll walk back to Josh's. I need the fresh air.'

When she stepped out of the front door he called after her, 'I won't say anything, Rose. Not till we get back to London.'

Rose headed away, walking swiftly along. Then she turned on to the Promenade, her head down, her thoughts muddled. She did not want to think about the things she had just read. She glanced at the sea. It looked muddy and flat, the sky a dirty white. After a while she turned off the front and headed for Joshua's house. Turning into the street she almost came to a full stop.

The silver SUV was parked further down. There was a woman sitting in the driver's seat as there had been the previous day. She slowed down and looked again to see if the dog was there too.

It was. A small Jack Russell type of dog.

So what, if a woman wanted to sit in her SUV in the middle of the day two days in succession? She might have any number of reasons for that. Rose would not become paranoid. She should look at things sensibly. Approaching the SUV, she took a good look at the woman behind the steering wheel. The only thing she could see for sure was that she had short white-blonde hair. The woman seemed to move as if she knew Rose was looking. Rose made a dramatic tutting sound and looked down at her laces. She knelt on one knee and fiddled with the other shoelace. At the same time she looked at the SUV and saw the first letters in its registration – *GT50 D* . . . She closed her eyes and memorised it. G for Gold, T for Tango, 50 for golden wedding anniversary, D for Delta. She said it over and over in her head for a few seconds then stood up again.

She walked past the car and went into Joshua's house.

SIX

Just after two Rose had a call from Joshua.

'Can you come down to the seafront? There's a cafe at the far end. It's the first turn after the pub, about twenty metres down. It's the Blue Kettle. There's someone I need to see there.'

'Sure,' Rose said. 'I'll get my coat and be there in ten minutes or so.'

Rose was relieved to be going out. She'd spent the last couple of hours on Facebook and then read some downloads for college work. She was fed up and needed some fresh air.

The Blue Kettle sat between a chemist's and a charity shop. It was painted blue and the name was pretty but the window was covered with a thin wire mesh which suggested that it had been broken or had graffiti sprayed on to it at some time or other. The heat hit her as she opened the door. Joshua was sitting at a table by the wall reading a newspaper. There were half a dozen other people but the place did not look busy.

'I'll get a drink,' she said. 'You want one?'

He shook his head, pointing to the mug in front of him.

She bought a peppermint tea and sat down opposite him.

'Everything all right?' she said.

'I saw Stu. He's more awake now but he says he doesn't remember anything about the fall. He's a little bit out of it really. I didn't feel I could ask him about the thing with Susie or why he was drinking. And I certainly didn't tell him about the newspaper report.'

'There'll be plenty of time to go through all that when he's better.'

'Yeah, I know. But I don't know how long that will take. He's in a bad way. He says his head hurts.'

'He banged it in the fall. It's bound to hurt.'

'You're right. I just . . . When I first heard that he fell I didn't really think about the actual consequences. I was just glad that he was alive. But seeing him now I realise how badly injured he is.'

'You can't fall off a cliff and walk away.'

'Anyway,' he said after a few moments, 'I went to the police station and met this officer, Joe Warner. He's an old friend of Stu's. He's one of those community police officers who go into schools and give talks about drugs and stuff. So he's been looking into the fall, trying to find out what happened. He's looked at the CCTV footage in the parking area near the cliff walk at Cullercoats. There's no footage of Stu's car because for some reason he parked in a street nearby. Maybe that's another reason why he wasn't missed. A car left overnight in the cliff car park might have raised an alarm. There is footage of a parked car, though, and a man getting out and walking towards the cliff path. Most of the car registration plate is visible and at one point the face of the driver can be seen. This was at about nine.'

'Do they know who it is?'

'He didn't say but his phone rang while he was talking to me. He turned away to have a conversation and I looked at the printout in front of him. The name on it was Greg Tyler.'

'Susie's husband?'

It made sense suddenly why they were sitting in the Blue Kettle. Rose looked up at the counter but there were only two women serving. Susie Tyler had said her husband was a partner in the business, which wasn't doing very well.

'Joe said they were talking to the man to see if he saw anything of the accident.'

'Why? Do they think there's more to it?'

Joshua shrugged his shoulders.

Just then the cafe door opened and a man came in looking flustered. He was talking on his mobile phone saying, 'I gotta go.' He was in his thirties, with longish hair. He was wearing a denim jacket which looked too tight. He took it off as he walked towards the counter and went through a door at the side. Moments later he was in front of the counter, his clothes covered up with a white apron.

'That might be him,' Joshua said.

'What are you going to do?'

'I'm going to talk to him.'

Joshua got up and walked across to the counter. He said something to Greg Tyler and the man frowned. Joshua continued talking and then turned and came back to the table.

'He's not exactly happy but he's coming over in five minutes.'

A while later Greg Tyler was sitting beside Rose, opposite Joshua. He was upright in the chair, not touching the table. In his hand he had his mobile and was glancing at it.

'What can I do for you?' he said abruptly.

'I want to know what you were doing at Cullercoats on Wednesday night when my uncle fell.'

'Been talking to the law?'

Joshua nodded. The man looked uncomfortable.

'Look, for obvious reasons I don't like your uncle. Susie said she told you everything when she brought your dog back. When me and your uncle had that fight in Morrisons I thought that was it, that he'd leave her alone. Then on Wednesday lunchtime I get a call from him. He wants to see me to talk things through. He tells me to meet him in the car park at Cullercoats that evening at nine thirty. I don't want to do it. He's the last person in the world I want to see but I was afraid he'd contact Susie so I told him I'd go. I get there early about nine. I sit in the car getting het up, angry. I get out of the car and decide to walk a bit to calm myself down.'

Greg Tyler's voice had risen. He seemed to notice it and carried on in lower tones. Rose leant forward to hear.

'Then I hear some voices from further up the path. I went a bit closer and I see the dog running round. Two men were standing facing each other. At first I thought they were talking but when the voices got louder I see that they were arguing. Then one of them pushed the other. I stood back because I realised it was Stuart Johnson. I didn't want him to see me. The other fellow walked off and Stuart was calling after him. Then he went after him.'

He stopped as if expecting Joshua to say something.

'To tell you the truth I'd cooled down by then and I was glad for a reason to scoot off. I left. I got back to my car and drove home, never said a word to Susie about it, nothing. Next day Susie comes into the cafe, in front of the girls here, and tells me that Stuart Johnson fell off the cliff. No one was more surprised than me.'

'Why didn't you go to the police then? Tell them you saw Stu with this guy?'

Greg Tyler stood up.

'I don't have to justify myself to you.'

'Don't you care? He probably fell off the cliff when you were there.'

'He should have left my wife alone. Then I might have cared.'

He walked back to the counter. Rose looked round and saw him go in the side door. Then he reappeared on the other side.

'I'm going,' Joshua said, bristling. 'Otherwise I'll end up shouting at him.'

Joshua walked away. Rose called after him.

'I'll just be a minute.'

The cafe door shut and she turned and saw Greg Tyler staring after him. She took a deep breath and walked up to the counter.

'What?' he said bad-temperedly.

'I just want to ask you one thing. Did you see the man that Stuart Johnson was arguing with?'

'Who are you, *Dr Watson*?'

'Please. We're just trying to find out what happened.'

'You his girlfriend?' he said.

Rose shook her head. 'Stepsister. Sort of . . .'

'I didn't see the guy. It was pitch dark up there. Johnson knew him, though. He called him by name, Len or Ben or Den, something like that.'

'Thanks,' she said.

'It wasn't my fault. I mean about him and my wife. I can't be blamed for that!'

'No, I understand. Josh is upset. He's just been to see him. He's in a bad way.'

For the first time Greg Tyler looked a little shamefaced.

'Falling off a cliff. It's not recommended.'

She walked away from the counter, feeling hot and puffed up. Opening the door she was glad of the cold air. Joshua was across the road, leaning back against a brick wall, waiting for her. She walked over and stood in front of him. He was staring at the Blue Kettle, his face hard.

'You can't blame him for being negative about your uncle.'

'*Negative?* What a polite way you have of talking, Rosie!'

Rose looked away. It wasn't like Joshua to snap at her.

'I'm sorry. I'm just amazed that he can talk about him so . . . When he was most probably *there* when he fell. Come on. Let's not hang round here. Let's go back to the house.'

They began to walk slowly as if they didn't really have anywhere to go. People passed by and they had to go single file. The Promenade seemed to be in shadow, heavy clouds in the sky. Rose waited for Joshua to get level with her and then she linked her arm through his.

'Oh,' she said. 'Greg Tyler said that your uncle called out the man's name. The man he was arguing with.'

Joshua nodded.

'He said it was Den or Len or maybe Ben.'

Joshua frowned.

'Did your uncle know someone with one of those names?'

Joshua stiffened as though something had just clicked inside his head.

'What? Are those names familiar?'

'No,' Joshua said. 'But they sound a lot like *Bren*.'

Rose frowned. 'Bren?'

'Stu called my dad Bren. It was his name for him.'

'Bren? I don't get it.'

'Maybe it was my *dad* that Stu was arguing with. Maybe my *dad* was here in Newcastle on Wednesday night!'

SEVEN

By the time they got back to the house Joshua was certain that his uncle had been talking to his dad on the night of his fall. On top of that he had convinced himself that they had been in touch with each other during the whole five years since he disappeared.

'It makes sense,' he said. 'I don't know why I didn't think of it before. As soon as we found out that Dad and Kathy were alive I should have worked it out. If Dad was alive then Stu would know something about it.'

The minute they got in he decided he wanted to search the house. Rose wasn't convinced. The reasoning was so slim.

'What exactly are you looking for?' Rose said.

'I don't know. Evidence of some recent communication between Dad and Stu. Some paperwork or Dad's belongings, maybe things he asked Stu to look after. Anything that shows that they've been in touch with each other.'

Joshua looked different. He had come alive, as if a fire had been lit inside him. She watched as he rang Skeggsie and explained breathlessly what Greg Tyler had said. When he ended the call Rose could just imagine that Skeggsie would drop everything and come round.

Ten minutes later he was at the door. Then Joshua got organised.

'Rosie, you take the living room and the kitchen. Skeggs, you look at Stu's computer and I'll do the study and Stu's bedroom and the upstairs in general. Rosie, you need to look under things, see if the carpet's been lifted up. Be thorough.'

'But do you really think . . .'

Rose heard them go up the stairs and then the sound of Poppy following them. She looked around the kitchen with consternation. One word had made this come about. One word that possibly was a mishearing of something called out at a distance. Ben, Len or Den.

She walked wearily to the sink and ran some water on to her fingertips. She pressed them around her eyes. Then she sighed and started to search. She stood on the kitchen chairs and looked on the top of all the cupboards. Then she searched through each cupboard, moving everything around in case something had been secreted beneath. What the *something* was she wasn't sure but still she wanted to be thorough. From above there was the sound of furniture being moved about, drawers opening and closing. She continued moving dishes and pots, looking into dark corners, feeling around in places she couldn't actually see. The kitchen drawers were messy and she pulled out a wad of stuff, mostly leaflets from pizza delivery companies and Indian takeaways.

The one thing she found was a small diary. Flicking through, she found empty page after empty page. Nothing had been written in it. It was an odd thing for a man to have. It was the kind of diary that fitted into a handbag. Possibly it had been a Christmas present from one of Stu's students and he hadn't wanted to throw it away.

The living room search seemed easier. She pulled the sofa out and looked at the carpet to see if it had been lifted but there was no sign that anything had been moved. There were a couple of shelves of books and she painstakingly took each one down and held it by its spine. Nothing dropped out. She moved ornaments and then looked with dismay at three shelves of DVDs. Her shoulders slumped. The only way to be sure was to look through each of them. She sat cross-legged on the floor and took each one out and searched through it. Then she ran her fingers along the back of each shelf to see if anything was stuck or wedged there. She put the DVDs back.

It had quietened down upstairs and Rose wondered if Joshua was going through Stu's paperwork, a much more difficult job than the one she was doing. There would be more books and files and ring binders.

She still wasn't sure exactly *what* they were looking for.

When she was sure there was nothing in the living room she went back into the hallway. Underneath the stairs there was a cupboard. She opened it. Several coats were hung up there. She took each one out and searched the pockets. She found packets of tissues, several half-finished packets of Lockets and some chewing gum. She found small black plastic bags, which he must have taken out on his walks with Poppy. She also found, to her embarrassment, a packet of condoms. She closed the cupboard door and suddenly felt tired.

How long had this search been going on? An hour, more like two? She went into the kitchen and made a cup of tea. While the rumblings went on upstairs she sat down to drink it and picked up the pocket diary and looked through it. There was nothing at all written in it. She let the pages flick back and forth and then something caught her eye. It was a date that had been circled – 24th June. In the otherwise blank pages the simple blue circle stood out and she wondered how she could have missed it. She flicked through and saw that other dates had been circled – 24th January, 24th February, 24th August. One day every month had been marked. No explanation, no written note as to why. It reminded Rose of the days when she'd been a student at Mary Linton boarding school and girls used to circle dates in their diaries to indicate that their period was due.

The day circled in this diary was always the twenty-fourth. Why had Stu marked these days out? The last one of the year was due to come up soon. Monday 24th December, Christmas Eve.

The kitchen door opened and Poppy appeared, her tail wagging, her tongue hanging out. The dog looked weary as though she had been searching as well. Rose huffed. It sounded as though they were still busy upstairs. She stood up.

'Want to go for a walk?'

Poppy followed her out to the hall. She picked up her coat and the lead and then shouted up the stairs.

'I'm finished searching, Josh. I'm taking the dog for a walk.'

From a distance she heard a sound. It might have been *OK* or *All right*.

She headed towards the seafront. After a few minutes she turned on to the Promenade and felt the force of the wind off the North Sea. She made for the beach. The wind made her stop and she swayed. The smell of brine was strong, the wind damp, droplets of seawater carried by the rushing air. She walked along, the dog's lead extending and retracting as Poppy found things to rush at. Then she stood very still looking out at the waves, her hair blowing straight back off her face. The cold air woke her up and she kept going towards a covered bench at the end of the Promenade. It had seats on two sides, one facing the sea, the other facing the shops. It was too cold to look out to sea so she sat looking towards the street.

There were a lot of people milling about. She wondered if they were getting last-minute Christmas presents. She sat back and found herself watching a group of young people standing in front of a fried chicken outlet. They were huddled together, several of them smoking, one cupping his lighter to protect the flame. Two of the girls seemed to be singing something, their lips syncing some words that Rose couldn't make out. Their delight in the song made Rose smile. One of the girls was familiar and she remembered that she'd seen her in the pub the night before with Rory Spenser.

A voice startled her.

'Hi.'

She looked up and saw Martin, Joshua's friend.

'Hello,' she said.

He sat down beside her, dumping a couple of bags on the seat. Then he used both hands to pat and rub Poppy.

'How's Stuart?' he said.

'OK, I think. Have you been Christmas shopping?' she said.

'Mostly.'

'Is it always this cold here?'

'You mean here in the north or here by the sea?'

'By the sea.'

'This is nothing. This is mild.'

'What's it like in York? One of the tutors at my college says it's a great place to go.'

'It's definitely warmer there. Not. You should look it up. The uni is great and there's lots of nightlife. You could come up for a weekend. I'll show you round.'

'Do you always invite strange girls to come for a weekend?'

'I *only* invite strange girls. Ordinary ones are no fun.'

Rose smiled. She wasn't feeling so chilled now that the covered bench was shielding her from the wind.

'Do you always wear black?'

'I don't just wear black,' she said. 'I wear white as well.'

Today, though, she was all in black. Black roll-neck, jeans and boots.

'Funereal. Is this your general approach to life?'

'No, I wear black and white because those are the colours that I feel comfortable in. I'm fed up with people like . . . like Anna, my grandmother, telling me to wear colours because it's not what I want to do. Black and white has a kind of simplicity, a sharpness.'

'It's like you and me then. We go well together.'

'How do you mean?'

'You're white and I'm black.'

He let his hand hover over hers. His skin was like dark wood, hers as pale as paper.

'You are nice to look at,' he said.

He was staring at her and she shook her head.

'I'm not one of those girls you have to give compliments to,' she said, moving a little away from him. 'I don't need anyone to tell me how I look.'

'Everyone needs someone to tell them how they look. You look nice. Take the compliment. Don't throw it back at me.'

'OK,' she said after a moment's quiet. 'I'll take it.'

'There. That wasn't so bad, was it?'

She smiled. It wasn't so bad.

'Would you like to come for a drink with me? Tonight?'

She looked at him with surprise.

'What have I said?' he said.

She smiled and looked around, embarrassed.

'Is there something wrong with me?'

'No, no! I'm just . . . I don't . . . It's not a good time . . .'

'Ah! There's someone else, isn't there? You've left a boyfriend back in London.'

'No! Well . . .'

'Look, if you change your mind I'll be in the Lighthouse round seven. There'll be a bottle of beer with your name on it.'

'I doubt I'll be able to . . .'

He stood up. 'I'll be there if you change your mind . . .'

He walked off, his bags swinging. She couldn't help but smile.

Lighten up, Rose! she thought. *You just got asked out on a date!*

She watched him walk away. He stopped for a moment and spoke to the girl she'd recognised from the previous evening. They talked for a few minutes and then Martin disappeared into a shop. Michelle moved on and Rose's eyes followed her as she turned into the car park of a large hotel, the Royal. Michelle skipped straight up the steps to the entrance and went inside. Rose wondered if she worked there. Just then a woman came out of the swing doors holding a dog in her arms. She was tall and slim with white-blonde hair. When she reached the bottom step she let the dog jump down to the ground. Then she held out some car keys and Rose looked round and saw the sidelights on a silver SUV flick on and off.

It was the same SUV that she had seen in Joshua's street two days running. The driver was obviously a guest at the hotel. The woman got into the car with the dog. Moments later the SUV swept out of the car park and she saw the registration *GT50 DNT*. She was thoughtful as she watched it drive away from the Promenade.

Back at the house Skeggsie opened the door. She unhooked the dog's lead. Joshua was coming down the stairs. He didn't look as happy as he had earlier.

'Where've you been? You've been gone for ages!'

'Sorry, I finished searching and thought I'd take the dog out. Did you find anything?'

'No. We haven't searched everything yet and Skeggsie has still got a lot of files to go through on the computer.

We thought we'd take a break, get something to eat and carry on later.'

'Did you see the diary I found? I left it on the kitchen table.'

'No.'

She went to the kitchen and picked up the small book and handed it to Joshua.

'There's no writing in it, just dates that have been circled. I don't know what it means. It's the twenty-fourth of every month.'

'Why didn't you bring this upstairs as soon as you found it? These dates might signify something on Stu's computer. Why on earth did you just leave it here?'

'I wasn't sure if it was important.'

'You could have asked!'

'I was busy looking . . .'

'You could have asked, Rosie. You could have made an effort. I don't want to have to do everything by myself.'

Joshua took the diary and walked out of the kitchen. The door closed behind him. Skeggsie was looking awkward.

'I didn't think it was . . .'

'He's just upset. The possibility of his dad being in Newcastle has thrown him.'

Rose nodded wearily. She was becoming accustomed to having her head bitten off by Joshua.

EIGHT

The search continued all afternoon and evening. They spread out from the house and looked in the garage, the garden shed and the loft space. There was no sign of anything to do with Brendan in any of Stuart's belongings or papers. About nine o'clock they sat in the living room with cans of beer. On the coffee table was a blue file with letters spilling out of it.

'It hasn't been a complete waste of time,' Joshua said, sighing. 'I've found out that my uncle has major credit card debt.'

'How much?' Skeggsie said.

'The file's a mess but there are two accounts maxed out. Looks like almost eight thousand pounds. Most of it on online gambling. The bulk of it in the last four weeks.'

'Oh.'

'So on top of being heartbroken he also has no money.'

If only Joshua had visited his uncle, Rose thought, but did not say. A short weekend visit halfway through the term would have alerted Joshua that something was up. Maybe he would have found out that Susie was married and been able to say something to his uncle, to make him think. Or possibly he might have found some of the credit card bills and realised that something was wrong. Instead his uncle, free of anyone's disapproval, seemed to have nosedived, getting more deeply involved with Susie and sucked into debt.

But Joshua had been completely preoccupied with the search for their parents and had hardly ever mentioned his uncle and Rose had never thought to ask. Now he was going over and over it, coming back time and again to Greg Tyler's assertion that Stuart had called out the name *Bren*. Events were repeating themselves. His search for their parents was pushing Stuart aside again.

Rose was tired and still bruised by his sharp words that afternoon. She took a gulp of beer and decided she didn't feel like drinking any more. She said she'd have an early night and Joshua ummed and continued his conversation with Skeggsie.

The next morning as she opened the curtains in her room she saw the SUV again. It was there, parked further along on the other side of the street and the woman was sitting in the driver's seat. She couldn't see the dog but she guessed it was probably in the car.

Why was it there?

Was she being paranoid?

Joshua was downstairs. She could hear the radio and she could smell food cooking so she went into his room.

It was the first time she had been in there and she was surprised at how bare it was. It was as if he'd taken absolutely everything to London with him. There were no pictures on the wall, no ornaments, awards, photographs or memorabilia. How different it was to his London flat, which was full to bursting with posters, books, CDs, DVDs, magazines. It was as if he'd decided he wasn't coming back. She wondered, for a moment, if his uncle had seen it like that. If he had walked into the bare room and realised that Joshua, who had grown up with him, hadn't just gone to university. He'd gone for good.

Joshua's bag was in the corner still packed. The zip gaped and clothes spilled out as if he had rummaged round for any old thing to wear. Over the back of Joshua's bedside chair was the bomber jacket he'd bought for his uncle as a Christmas present. His laptop, phone, wallet and some papers were all strewn on the floor by his bed.

On the back of the door hung Joshua's new coat. Rose listened hard in case he was about to come upstairs. There was no sound so she thrust her hand into the pocket of the coat and pulled out the small notebook he'd been using to write down car registration numbers. She opened it and saw page after page of numbers written crookedly, some in pencil, some in pen. Each page had a date at the top. She sat down on the very edge of Joshua's bed and looked down the list. She started with the most recent, the day before yesterday when they'd been travelling up from London. *GT50 DNT* was what she was searching for.

Three-quarters of the way down she found it.

GT50 DNT.

She was right. The silver SUV was there when they stopped at the services. Surely that just was too much of a coincidence. She tore a piece of paper from the pad and wrote the number on it, shoving it into her pocket.

She looked down at the floor wondering what to do next. Joshua's things were by her feet, as if they'd just been thrown there. She picked all of it up, some papers falling away. She dropped everything on the duvet while she retrieved the papers from the floor. When she placed those alongside the wallet she saw that it had fallen open. On one half of it was a photograph. She was startled to see her own face.

Joshua carried a photo of her in his wallet.

She picked it up and saw that the photo was in one of the plastic pouches used for credit cards. She turned it over and there was Joshua's handwriting. *Rosie, Camden Market.* She remembered during their shopping trip earlier in the week Joshua had taken pictures with his phone. He must have cropped whatever shot it was to get this tiny image of her. And she wasn't even smiling. Her face had a quizzical look and her fringe was too long, dipping into her eyes. She was wearing the blue earrings so it must have been taken after he'd bought them for her.

She was surprised.

No, she was *touched* that he carried her picture with him.

Placing the wallet on the bedside table she remembered about the silver SUV. What was she going to do with the information? If she told Joshua it would only add to his worries. Skeggsie was due round soon. She'd wait until he was on his own and tell him. She replaced the notebook in Joshua's coat pocket.

Downstairs she went straight for the kettle. Joshua was sitting at the kitchen table reading things from his phone.

'You know what?' he said.

'What?' she said brightly, determined to start the day on a positive note.

She got some bread out and put a slice into the toaster.

'I've got this theory. I think Stu was in touch with Dad. Maybe the whole five years or maybe just part of it. Maybe once Dad was somewhere safe he contacted Stu telling him to keep the truth from me and Stu did that.'

Rose had her back to Joshua. She wanted to tell him to stop, to slow down, to forget the theories and just deal with his uncle's accident.

'I think that maybe Stu had some way of getting in touch with Dad; a number to ring, a PO box to write to.

Maybe he realised he was getting in a financial mess and asked him to meet him on Cullercoats Cliff. That's why he parked round the corner because he knew that any meeting with Dad had to be completely secret.'

'Why did he ask Greg Tyler to meet him there if he was meeting Brendan?'

'He was meeting Dad earlier, maybe eight thirty, and then he arranged for Greg to come later.'

'But would he do that if seeing Brendan was such a secret?'

'Rose, this is supposition. I'm just playing with ideas here. There's no need to squash it before I've even got it all out.'

'Sorry.'

'So he meets Dad and asks him for money and that's why they row. Or something.'

'And then?'

'And then Dad goes off.'

'And Greg Tyler? You think they met? You think he was telling the truth?'

'Maybe. No. I'm not sure.'

'If Stu wanted money, why not contact Brendan? Money can be moved by phone.'

'Ah,' Joshua smiled, on surer footing now. 'There's no way that Dad's going to transfer money from one bank account to another. There's a trail there that could lead back to him.'

'That's if Stuart was calling out Bren and not Ben, or Den, or Len.'

'Like I said it's just a theory.'

Joshua closed his eyes. He looked irritated.

'Don't talk to me about this,' Rose said sharply, 'if you don't want me to have an open and honest conversation with you. I'm not some kid you have to get annoyed at.'

'This isn't *about* you, Rose.'

'I know. I haven't talked about *me*. I'm trying to respond to what you said!'

Rose left her toast on the plate and walked out of the room. She felt incensed. It wasn't about *her*. She hadn't meant it that way! She walked up and down the hall for a few moments until she calmed down. Then she turned to go back to the kitchen but suddenly couldn't face sitting with Joshua, going round and round in circles. She actually had something important to tell him. She needed to let him know about the SUV but that would probably bring about some other barbed comments. *Why didn't you tell me before?* Or *Why are you bringing that up when there are other more important things to worry about?*

She picked up the door keys from the hall table and went outside. She looked up the street. The SUV was still there. She walked a few steps along the pavement and stood in full view staring at the driver. The woman stared back. The car was too far away to see her face but she sensed that the woman was concentrating on her. Then she saw the dog's face on the passenger side. Rose crossed her arms and stood very still. A couple of women passing by had to get round her and said, ''Scuse me, pet.' The woman's arm reached across to the dog. Then seconds later Rose heard the engine start and the indicator clicked. The car moved out and went down the street, gathering speed gradually. The driver's profile never flinched as the car passed her. When it was gone Rose felt herself relax suddenly.

She turned and saw Skeggsie coming towards her.

She put her hand in her back pocket and pulled out the piece of paper with the registration number on it.

'What you doing out here?' Skeggsie said.

'It's a long story. Could you ask your dad to find out about this registration number?'

She held out the piece of paper.

'How come?' he said, taking it.

'It's a silver SUV, like the one that Josh and I had dealings with in Stiffkey. It must have been parked in the services where we stopped on the way up. The first stop. And it's been parked in the street for short periods ever since. I think it might be following us. I didn't want to tell Josh in case I'm wrong or it winds him up more.'

'I'll see what *I* can do. There's a couple of programmes I've got for ferreting information out. If I can't then I'll ask Dad.'

'I don't think you should mention it to Josh yet. He's not in a good place.'

'I know.'

'Do you think that Brendan was here talking to Stuart on the night of the accident?'

Skeggsie blew between his teeth.

'Maybe. We know Brendan's alive, right?'

'And my mum.'

''Course. We know they're both alive. Why would Brendan not be in some sort of contact with Stuart? He is his brother and he's looking after his son.'

'But would Stuart keep it from Josh?'

'If Brendan asked him to. If the reason he disappeared is important enough. Yes, I think he would.'

Joshua appeared at the door. He looked at both of them sternly.

'When you two have finished with the small talk maybe we can get on? I've got to go to the hospital at eleven and then see Joe Warner!'

Rose met Skeggsie's eyes and exhaled slowly. She followed him up the path and into the house.

NINE

In the afternoon Rose and Joshua took Poppy for a walk.

Skeggsie was seeing relatives so they got the bus along Broadway for four stops until they got to Cullercoats. Then it was a short walk to the cliffs.

Joshua was in a better mood. At the hospital his uncle had been sitting up in bed sipping a drink, he said. He was still a bit groggy but seemed to remember the fact that he'd had too much to drink just before the fall.

'You didn't say anything to him about Brendan?' Rose said.

Joshua shook his head.

The policeman, Joe Warner, had been at the hospital talking to Stuart. On the way out, after the visit, he'd been positive. He'd told Joshua to give it time and that if there was anything to find out the police would do it. He'd also told him to try and get through Christmas.

'Shall I come and see him with you?' Rose said.

'That'd be nice. Come on Christmas Day.'

It was almost two o'clock and they were walking along the cliff path. It was cold and overcast. Rose had her hands in her pockets and her jacket zipped up to the neck. Behind them were the ruins of a castle. On their right was the sea, vast and calm. On the left was green parkland and the road beyond. In front the cliff walk snaked away from them. It was early afternoon but there was a hint of darkness over to the east. They walked on, Poppy dashing ahead, sniffing here and there, running in spurts and stopping, looking back then heading on.

'Poppy won't go near the edge?' Rose said.

'No, we've done this walk dozens of times. She knows the way.'

'Are you sure you're all right? Doing the walk won't upset you?'

'I want to do it. I want to see the place where Stu fell.'

Ten minutes or so later they came to a noticeboard that had been erected by the police.

Cliff Fall. A man had a cliff fall here on Wednesday 19th December at approx. 22.00 hours. He was not discovered until the morning on Thursday 20th. Did you see or hear anything unusual or suspicious along the cliff path during the evening of 19th December?

At the bottom was a telephone number to ring.

Joshua walked past the notice until he got to the edge.

Rose followed him. It wasn't as high as she had pictured it. The beach below could be clearly seen and between the cliff edge and the sand were two ledges that stuck out, like small shelves.

'Stu must have lain there all night,' Joshua said. 'See, if you're on the beach, you can see it. Not in the dark of course but it's clear now.'

'And Poppy?'

'Joe said they found her sitting up here. She was very cold. They wrapped her in silver blankets and took her to the vet. Susie Tyler picked her up from there.'

Joshua turned and looked away from the sea towards the park and the houses and the road.

'My dad could have parked anywhere along here and caught up with Stu while he was walking. That's what I've been thinking, Rose. You asked, this morning, why Stu would make an arrangement to meet my dad if he knew he was meeting Greg Tyler? It was a completely sensible thing to say. But what if Stu hadn't made that arrangement with my dad? What if he was meeting Greg here and my dad, for some reason of his own, *followed* him, thinking he was just out for a walk with the dog, called to him and they had a conversation that ended in a row. What if that happened?'

'That's possible,' Rose said.

Joshua continued looking at the area as though he was watching a replay of the events of the previous Wednesday night.

'Dad calls out to him. They talk. They argue about something, I don't know what. Then Dad walks away, in a huff and Stu calls after him, *Bren! Bren!* But Dad doesn't come back. Stu is upset. Don't forget he's already drunk a lot and he turns and walks straight on, like he would on the path only he's not on the path – he's on a diagonal from the road to the edge and before he knows it he just goes over.'

Joshua's voice was firm.

'It could have happened like that. Trouble is it raises so many questions. Was Stu in touch with Dad? Why? And why would Dad come to meet him here, anyway? Why not ring him or meet him at the house? I was away in London so there was no chance I'd walk in on them.'

Rose pulled at his arm and they walked on. Up ahead was a building that looked like it had seen better days. As they came to it she could see that there was a seating area in front of it as though it had once been a cafe. There were a couple of young men there. She recognised one of them. Rory Spenser was sitting beside another young man. There were cans of drink on the table in front of them. She felt Joshua stiffen. Poppy ran off in their direction. Rory got up and walked towards the dog, bending over to make a fuss of her. Rose tensed.

'All right, Josh?' Rory called.

Joshua gave a curt nod of his head. He held the lead up to Poppy and she reluctantly walked back towards them.

Rory stood very still, staring at them. The other young man never moved, just continued to drink out of his can. As soon as Joshua got Poppy back on the lead he turned and began to walk away. Rose followed him.

'Why are you still so angry at that boy?'

'Rory? Or his brother, Sean?'

'Rory. Martin said he'd changed.'

'Martin's an optimist. People like Rory don't change.'

His voice had become hard and he was walking swiftly. She had to quicken her step to keep up with him.

'Was that his brother?'

'Sean Spenser, an equally nasty piece of work. He taught Rory everything he knows.'

Rose linked her arm through his, pulling him back a little, trying to slow him down. They walked for a while in silence passing the point where the police notice was. Joshua's mood was all over the place. One minute he was calmly talking about his dad, the next he was angry at Rory Spenser, some boy from the past. He was like someone flailing about in deep water, grabbing at anything to keep himself from going under.

'Martin's nice,' she said, changing the subject.

'He's a good mate.'

'He asked me on a date!'

She stopped. *Rose, Rose, why did you say that*, she thought.

'What?'

'I saw him yesterday when I took Poppy for a walk and he, he just asked me out.'

'Are you going to go?'

Joshua was looking straight at her, puzzled.

''Course not,' she said, steering him away from bumping into a signpost at the end of the path.

He was quiet as they walked along the pavement back towards the bus stop. Then he pulled her to a halt.

'Rosie, you don't have to say no to Martin because of all this stuff about Stu . . .'

'I don't want to go . . .' she said.

The bus was coming now and they both ran for it. They got on, breathless and found a seat near the front. Joshua didn't say any more about Martin and Rose, relieved, looked out of the window, her eye catching the Royal hotel as they passed it.

Later, in the evening, Skeggsie came round with fish and chips and they watched a DVD that he'd brought. There was red wine and beer and Rose found herself drinking more than she'd meant to. Halfway through the film Josh got some whisky out of a drinks cabinet and asked if anyone else wanted some. Neither she nor Skeggsie did. Joshua left the bottle at his side and kept refilling his glass. When they said goodbye to Skeggsie Joshua was unsteady on his feet, his words a little slurred. He sat back down in his seat and Rose walked to the door with Skeggsie.

'I've never seen Josh drunk,' she said.

'I have. He'll sleep it off.'

'Did you have any luck with the registration number?'

He shook his head. 'Trying a couple of Incision Programmes.'

'What?'

'Taking data out of secure files without anyone noticing. Eddie's helping me down in London. I will ask Dad but as a last resort. I don't want him poking his nose into our business.'

'Would he be angry?'

'No, he'd just take it over!'

The door closed and Rose went into the kitchen. She poured herself another tumbler of red wine and returned to the living room. She sat watching television for a while, feeling the wine warming up her throat. She looked over at Joshua and saw that he had fallen asleep. He was still sitting up in the armchair but his head was lolling forward. She put her wine down and stood up. She would have to move him, get him up to bed. She shoved at his arm.

'Josh, time for bed, Josh. JOSH.'

His eyes opened and with difficulty she pulled him up to a standing position.

'We're going to go upstairs now, Josh, come on. One foot after the other.'

'Thaks . . .' he said, one arm around her shoulder.

She manoeuvred him out of the room and then they took the stairs carefully one at a time, resting between steps. Rose was cajoling him to keep going and finally, at the top of the stairs, she lifted his arm from around her shoulder and pulled him towards his bedroom. He staggered towards the bed, sat down and fell sideways, his head on the pillow, his eyes closed, his feet still on the floor.

She turned on the bedside lamp and it gave the room a dull yellow glow. It was a double bed and Joshua was slumped on one edge of it. Rose picked his feet up and laid him out. Then, putting the flats of her hands under his waist, she pushed him so he rolled over and lay on his side in the middle of the bed. Then she sat on the edge of the bed, tired with the effort. Maybe she'd drunk a little too much red wine herself.

'Thaks, Rosie,' she heard him whisper from behind her.

Her shoulders relaxed and she let herself flop back down on the bed. It was only for a moment. She could hear the television from downstairs and she knew she had to turn everything off and let Poppy out into the garden before she went to bed herself. She lifted her feet off the floor. She turned to the side. Joshua was completely still beside her. She lay quietly for a while then put her arm around him so that her hand was on his chest. She felt his ribs move up and down.

His T-shirt had risen up. She saw the edge of his tattoo. Like hers it was of a butterfly. She pushed her sleeve up to expose her own. They both had the same tattoos; it seemed like a private link between them.

Joshua stirred. She stiffened, thinking she ought to move before he woke up and found her there. She lifted her arm gently and went to turn away but Joshua's hand covered hers and pulled her back. He seemed to hold her there.

'Josh?' she whispered.

There was no answer. He was still asleep. She should move and yet his hand was warm over hers and she had curled herself into the crook of his back. She closed her eyes for just a moment, feeling her chest against him. The wine was taking its toll and she was feeling tired. Joshua was so still, as if all the worries of the last few days had left him. She let her face sink into his neck, his hair tickling her nose. He smelled of shampoo and soap and whisky.

He moved her hand a little.

Was he asleep?

'Rosie,' he seemed to say.

He had her fingers tightly in his and he moved them upwards until they reached his face. Then he kissed her wrist, slowly, softly, his tongue on her skin.

A feeling of yearning flooded through her. Hardly breathing, she put her mouth on his shoulder and kissed it, brushing it lightly, her lips like the touch of a feather. They lay still for a while then he seemed to drop her hand and become heavier, slumped, moving a little away from her. She edged back.

'Night, Josh,' she whispered.

She closed his door. She walked quickly to the box room and sat down on the bed, her arms hugging her chest. Her skin was tingling with desire.

What was going on? Did Joshua *want* her?

She wished she knew.

TEN

Christmas Eve brought snow.

Rose looked out of her bedroom window to see if the SUV was there and she was faced with a white scene. Snowflakes were floating down but not quite settling on the ground. She was relieved to see that the silver car was not in the street. She got dressed and went downstairs to let Poppy out into the garden. The cold air poured in and she shut the door quickly after the dog. She was thirsty and poured herself a glass of water and drank most of it down. It was just after nine thirty and there was no sound of movement from Joshua's room. She put the kettle on and got out some bread.

There was a knock at the front door.

She opened it to find a man of about fifty holding a cardboard box, the kind people used when they were moving house.

'Is Joshua Johnson in?'

She nodded.

'I'm Donald Bishop, the head teacher of Kirbymoore Academy where Stuart Johnson teaches history. Sorry to bother you on Christmas Eve but I wanted to get this stuff to Stuart in case any of it was needed over the holidays.'

'Oh.'

'May I come in?' he said, looking up at the falling snow.

'Of course.' She held the door back.

Donald Bishop walked in. She pointed towards the kitchen.

'If you go in there I'll tell Josh that you're here.'

'Thank you, dear.'

Rose ran up the stairs. She knocked on Joshua's door. She heard a mumble from inside the room. She opened it a fraction.

'Josh, Stu's head teacher is here. He's downstairs in the kitchen. He wants to see you.'

Joshua was completely covered by the duvet. He groaned.

'I'll make him a drink and tell him you're coming.'

She went downstairs. The dog was yapping at the back door. She let her in and she wagged her tail at Donald Bishop then ran out of the room and up the stairs.

'Please sit down. Josh will be five minutes.'

'I am rather early,' Donald Bishop said, 'but being Christmas Eve I had a few other errands to run. And you are?'

'I'm Rose, Josh's stepsister. Sort of.'

'You're looking after the lad, after this business. We heard about the accident on the last day of term and there was considerable upset among his classes.'

There was movement from upstairs, footsteps, doors opening and closing. Poppy had managed to get Joshua up. Rose was relieved.

'Let me make you a hot drink,' she said.

'That's very kind of you. Strong tea please with milk and two sugars.'

Moments later Joshua appeared at the kitchen door. He was dressed but looked unwell. Rose noticed the whisky bottle on the side. She quickly tucked it away in the cupboard as Donald Bishop began to speak to Joshua, saying more or less the same thing that he'd said to her earlier. She made Joshua a drink – milky coffee. Then she slipped out and went upstairs, leaving them to talk alone.

She paused at Joshua's room. His duvet was half hanging on to the floor. Just the previous evening she'd been lying on the bed beside him. Had he even known she was there? Or had he simply been in a drunken stupor?

She walked back to her room. From downstairs she could hear the mumble of voices coming from the kitchen. She felt tired and out of sorts. Maybe she also had a hangover.

In the corner of the small bedroom was the rucksack she had brought with her. It was a mess – clothes half pulled out of it, her toiletries scattered. She unzipped it entirely and tipped the contents on to the bed. She sorted through the myriad of stuff that fell out and found, in the middle, the gift that Anna had bought her for Christmas. She sat down on the single bed and opened it. It was a book and Anna had filled it with pictures of her mother. There was a folded piece of notepaper inside. *I found these among your mother's things. I thought you might like them.* Rose looked at them with a creeping sense of pleasure. There were about twenty. She flicked through them, family shots as well as photos of Kathy in her work clothes and with friends. There was even a picture of Kathy and Brendan standing together by a car.

She cleared her things from the bed and lay on her side and looked through the album.

She focused on the family shots. There were a couple of Christmas photos where her mother had a paper hat on. Then some of Rose and her mother in the garden at Brewster Road. She knew it was there because the garden had always been a bit of a jungle and they mostly used the top half of it where there was a stone patio. She kept thumbing through the pages, coming back to one picture in particular. Rose and her mother were sitting side by side on garden chairs. Her mother had an arm around Rose's shoulder. She was wearing dark glasses and was showing all her teeth in a cheesy grin as though someone, probably Brendan, had ordered her to smile. Rose looked closely at her own image. She was probably going on for twelve. The photo must have been taken during that last summer. Rose had left primary school and had spent time in the holidays shopping for her new uniform. During one of those shopping trips her mum had bought her a pair of cut-off jeans that had sequins sewn along the pockets and round the hem. *Cool jeans*, Joshua had said. Brendan had called her a fashionista. She was wearing them in the photo. She'd worn them every day for weeks. Every morning she got up and put them on pushing her feet into plimsolls or slip-ons. She loved them and wouldn't wear anything else, sitting around in her pyjama bottoms if her mum insisted on washing them. As soon as they were dry they went straight back on. Putting on the school uniform in September had been like a punishment. She'd kept the jeans in her drawer for the following summer but in between her family disintegrated and she ended up living at her grandmother's. The jeans had been folded among all her stuff, unpacked by Anna's cleaner and placed in her new chest of drawers. When she discovered them there weeks later it felt as though her chest would split apart with sadness. She marched downstairs and threw them into the dustbin at the side of the house. She couldn't bear the sight of them.

Rose turned the page, not wanting to become emotional. Some work photos showed Kathy with colleagues. Rose's eyes swept across them. She might have known some of them at the time. They might have been the people who rang up to speak to her mum or who came round for dinner parties clutching a bottle of wine. But it was so long ago that none of the faces rang any bells. She focused on one picture which she was sure must have been taken by Brendan although she couldn't explain why. Her mum was wearing a dark suit and her hair was pulled back at the base of her neck. She had make-up on and her glasses were straight and neat. There was only a hint of a smile on her lips as if she were doing her best to look serious. She was a police officer. She worked on cold cases. She was important and professional.

She looked from one to another, her mother's face smiling out from the past. For a few moments she felt all the pleasure of seeing her so close, like an unexpected meeting, a surprise reunion, and then there was the slow agonising awareness that this was just a mirage, that her mother was as far away from her as she had been for the last five years and more. The photos were just a cruel reminder of what she had once had.

Just then she heard the head teacher walking along the hallway downstairs. He was talking loudly like teachers do. Joshua's voice was just a whisper underneath it. The front door opened and closed. Rose went downstairs and found Joshua sitting at the kitchen table with his head in his hands.

'I don't feel well,' he said.

'Why don't you go back to bed for a few hours?'

He nodded.

'That's Stu's stuff from his locker at school,' he said, pointing at the cardboard box which was now on the floor. 'They're having building work or something and lockers had to be cleared.'

'I'll put it away,' Rose said.

Joshua went out of the room. After having some breakfast Rose carried the box up to Stuart's room. She went quietly so as not to wake Joshua. The room was untidy and Rose remembered that Joshua had searched it the previous day. There were piles of papers on the floor around Stuart's desk and the duvet was rumpled and crooked. She placed the box on top of the bed. She decided to unpack it. There were clothes and boots as well as books and files. She put them on the bed. She picked out two football team mugs and placed them on the bedside table. Underneath was a games console and a couple of chargers and some connection leads entangled. There were also a couple of clip frames with pictures of Joshua.

At the very bottom was a money box.

It felt like it was made from steel and was the size of a hardback book. She wondered if it was full of money, notes perhaps. It was locked but not heavy. She upended it and something moved inside. A single item slid from one end to the other. It didn't sound like cash. She placed it on the bed.

Then she went out on to the landing. There was silence from Joshua's room. She was feeling tired and a bit chilly.

She picked up the single duvet from her bed and went down, to the living room. She put on the television and lay on the sofa, covering herself up with the duvet. She gazed at the programmes, not really paying much attention. Every now and again she glanced over at the window and saw the snow drifting lazily down.

She dozed off to sleep.

'Rose, wake up, Rose!'

She jerked awake and saw Joshua standing in front of her holding something.

'I found this! Look, I found this in Stu's things.'

She sat up, her head ringing slightly. She glanced at the clock. It was almost midday. She'd slept for nearly two hours. Joshua was dressed and was holding the cash box she'd found earlier. It had its lid up.

'Look,' Joshua said, sitting down beside her. 'There was a key in Stu's desk that opened this.'

Inside the money box was a mobile phone. It was old-fashioned. It looked like pay as you go and Rose wondered what the fuss was about. Stu had an old mobile that he kept at school. So what?

'The battery was dead. I found a charger in among the other things you'd unpacked. Once I plugged it in I was able to access the data!'

Joshua was excited, running at full speed, but Rose was still heavy with sleep and dazed by being woken up in the middle of it. She took the mobile and looked at the screen. It showed *Call History*. There was a list of phone numbers, a couple of them the same but mostly they were different. She scrolled down it and saw that it went back to the previous January.

'Look at the dates!'

Each call was made on the same date. The twenty-fourth of every month – the same dates that were ringed in the diary that she had found. Except in December when there had been three extra calls.

'This is a phone that Stu kept locked away at work. There was no way I could stumble on this. He kept this phone for a single call that he got every month.'

'From different numbers.'

'Mostly.'

'Why don't you ring the numbers?'

'I was thinking that,' Joshua said, reaching for the mobile.

'Not on this phone. The number will show up.'

'You're right. I'll get my mobile.'

He went off. She heard him run up the stairs. Fully awake now, she threw the duvet back and put the mobile on the coffee table. She stretched her arms up and moved her shoulders.

It was twelve o'clock.

Suddenly the mobile rang. It startled her. The ringtone was like an old-fashioned telephone. She watched it for a second and then snatched it up.

'It's ringing,' she shouted.

There was no reply from upstairs and she let it ring another couple of times before pressing the receive button and putting the phone to her ear. She didn't speak.

'Stu, it's me,' a man's voice said. 'Stu, I'm sorry about the other night. I've got a lot on my mind at the moment.'

Rose felt her mouth go dry. She heard Joshua's footsteps come down the stairs. The man's voice continued.

'Stu, don't be pissed off. I'll try and sort some money out. I told you I wouldn't let you down.'

Joshua was in the room. He was looking at her quizzically.

'I thought we weren't going to make the calls on that phone?' he said.

Rose tried to block out Joshua's words. She turned away from him to concentrate on what was being said.

'For God's sake, Stu, grow up!'

'Who is this?' Rose said. 'Who's speaking?'

The phone went dead. She took it away from her ear.

'What?' Josh said.

But she couldn't speak to him. She had to write down what had been said before it went out of her head.

'I need a pen.'

In the kitchen she pulled the drawer open and scrabbled round to find a pen. Then she grabbed a junk mail envelope that was on the side. She started to write on it.

'What's going on, Rose?'

'Don't speak to me. Just for a minute. Don't say a word!'

She wrote the lines as she remembered them. Four times he spoke with gaps in between. Four lines. It wasn't verbatim but it was as clear as she could remember.

'Rose, WHAT?' Joshua said, looking angry.

'The phone rang at twelve o'clock. It was Brendan speaking.'

'Dad?'

'I'd swear to it. It was his voice, Josh. I'm sure it was. This is what he said. He must have thought it was Stuart who answered. Here's what he said. I wrote the words down as best I could.'

'My dad, on the phone? My *dad* spoke on that phone?'

'He did. He thought he was speaking to Stu.'

'What's the number? Read out the number to me. If I use a different phone he might answer.'

She read out the number on the screen.

Joshua punched it into his mobile and held it to his ear. His face was rapt, his shoulders tensed, rounded with anticipation. He was hoping to hear his dad's voice. She held her breath while he had the phone clamped to his ear. Then he lowered it. He seemed to deflate.

'No answer.'

'It was Brendan's voice. I know it was,' she said.

'I wish I could have heard it,' he whispered.

ELEVEN

An hour later Skeggsie came round. Rose was watching for him out of the window. For once she'd been the one to summon him. He'd been going out somewhere with his dad, he'd said, and would come later but she'd insisted. *You have to come now! This is important!*

She opened the door, relieved to see him. He had his hood up and shook off loose snow on to the doorstep before stepping into the hall.

'Thanks for coming,' she said.

Joshua was upstairs in his uncle's study. They could hear drawers opening and shutting. Earlier she'd followed him up there and tried to talk to him but he seemed frenetic, determined to search again, to take the place apart. She'd put her hand on his arm and said that they should sit down, have a hot drink, something to eat, think it through. But he shrugged her off and continued, dumping stuff on the floor, making piles of paper from places he'd already looked through.

It made her unhappy to see him like that.

That's why she had rung Skeggsie.

'He's been like this ever since I told him about the phone call.'

She followed Skeggsie into the kitchen. Looking around she noticed that the room was untidy, breakfast things not washed up. Skeggsie picked Stuart's mobile off the kitchen table and turned it over as if the answer was there inside it. He looked at the safe and the keys.

'How can you be so sure it was Brendan's voice?' he said.

'I know his voice. He lived with me for three years. I just know it was him.'

'And he rang at twelve, like a prearranged time.'

'On the twenty-fourth of every month.'

'Why circle the date in a diary? It's easy to remember.'

'Maybe he did that to identify which day of the week it fell on. Then he knew whether to have the phone here or at work.'

'Maybe.'

Skeggsie was thoughtful.

'This is weird. His uncle must know where Brendan is. Maybe Stu is a *part* of whatever it is.'

Whatever it is. The notebooks. Would they ever really know what it was?

Skeggsie walked up and down for a few moments. Rose saw he'd had his hair cut; razor cut, very short. It was just the way his new friend Eddie wore his hair. It made her feel funny for a second as if Skeggsie was edging away from them in some way. The sound of Joshua moving stuff around upstairs seemed louder and a little manic. It gave her a sense of growing unease. With Joshua like this, emotional and unstable, she needed Skeggsie around.

'You've had your hair cut,' she said pointlessly.

He gave a tiny shake of his head, dismissing the subject. He stopped moving around. He took his coat off and hung it round the back of the chair and rubbed his hands together in a businesslike way.

'I know we said we would postpone all this stuff about the notebooks until we got back to London but we can't now. Now that this has happened we have to face up to it. His Uncle Stuart is linked in some way.'

'Maybe the phone calls were simply Brendan trying to check that Joshua was well?'

'OK, but the fact is that Stuart knew that Brendan was alive and he kept it from Joshua. Why would he do that unless he knew why they'd disappeared? Unless he understood it all?'

'Because his brother asked him to?'

'But to lie to Josh? To pretend? There's a bigger reason for all this and we just don't know it yet. We have to tell Josh about the page I've decoded. And there's the SUV. If someone's following him it could mean danger of some sort. We can't let that happen again.'

Rose nodded. She didn't like to agree with Skeggsie but she knew he was right. She was concerned that these things were sending Joshua to the edge, maybe even out of control. They couldn't leave all this until they returned to London. It had literally followed them here.

'I'll get him down here. We can tell him this other stuff together. Then we'll have to make a plan.'

Skeggsie was bristling. He was always in his element when there were things to be done. It irked Rose and yet she had known he would be like this. She'd called him because he was utterly loyal and completely reliable. He was never happier than when he was doing something for Joshua. He went upstairs and she sat down and waited. After what seemed like a long time they came down talking quietly. When they got into the kitchen Joshua looked wrecked.

'What's going on?' he said.

Skeggsie showed him the page he'd decoded from the notebook. Rose read over Joshua's shoulder.

Operation VB
Viktor Baranski at an event in his restaurant, Eastern Fare, July 15 at 17.30.

She looked up at Skeggsie. He was staring at Joshua fiddling with his collar as he usually did when he was nervous. She focused on the paper again, at the important section.

Once in custody Baranski should be passed on to B.
Change cars.
B will take him to Stiffkey.
B will hand him over to F.
B will wait until operation is complete.
B will help dispose of evidence.

'I don't get it,' Joshua said.

'It seems to imply that Brendan was involved with the abduction of Viktor Baranski,' Skeggsie said bluntly.

Thank goodness Skeggsie didn't add his other concern – that Brendan had been somehow involved with the Russian secret service in the *killing* of Viktor Baranski. Rose knew that Joshua couldn't take that on top of everything else.

'And,' Skeggsie went on, 'Rose noticed that a car has been following us. It was at the services on the way up here and it was in the street outside for a couple of days. It's a silver SUV, registration number *GT50 DNT*. There was a woman sitting in it each time you saw it, isn't that right, Rose?'

'And a dog.'

Joshua looked at Rose.

'Why didn't you tell me?'

'I didn't want to worry you. You had enough on your mind.'

'Can we find out who owns the car?'

'I'm trying. Obviously, if I had my London hardware I could do it more quickly but I only have my laptop so it's taking time. I've been in touch with Eddie and he's helping.'

'This is all adding up to something I don't like,' Joshua said. 'My dad seems to have been part of something underhand. My uncle knew he was still alive and let me live here for five years without telling me.'

'Maybe it wasn't his choice,' Rose said softly. 'Maybe Brendan put pressure on him.'

Joshua shook his head. 'Stu was a strong bloke. He wouldn't have done anything he didn't want to. Maybe . . .'

'What?'

'Maybe he was part of it in some way.'

'How?'

'I don't know, Rosie!' Joshua said, his voice raised. 'If I knew exactly what happened to my dad then I'd have some idea of how he was involved.'

Rose flinched at his anger.

'And my mum,' she said, her voice breaking. 'Maybe if you stop thinking of your dad and your uncle then you might remember that my mum is part of this as well.'

'Hey! You two! This isn't getting us anywhere.'

'Sorry, Rosie,' Joshua said, reaching out and grabbing her hand. 'I just feel like I want to hit someone.'

'Not me?'

'No,' he smiled.

Skeggsie was standing by the table, holding the key ring up. Two keys hung down. He was looking closely at them.

'Keys to the money box,' Joshua said.

'There's two.'

'You always get a spare.'

'But they're two different keys.'

Joshua took the key ring from Skeggsie and held the two keys together.

'They are.'

'That might mean there's another box somewhere. Something else that your uncle has hidden. This must be the key for it.'

'But you've looked everywhere,' Rose said.

Joshua stood up. He dropped the two keys on the table.

'He's put it somewhere that he knows I will never look. Like *that* was in his school,' he said, pointing at the mobile phone.

'Where, though?'

'We looked in every single place. Unless . . .'

Joshua went out of the room and up the stairs. Skeggsie followed him. Rose went after them. He went into his uncle's bedroom and stood at one corner of his bed. With an effort he edged the bed to the side.

'Help me,' he said.

Skeggsie got to the other side.

'We'll pull it out as far as we can. I can get underneath. Maybe he's loosened the floorboards.'

It was a double bed and hard to shift. They edged it along as far as it would go, so that it was flat up against the wardrobe doors. Josh lay down on his stomach and slid under the bed.

'Get the bedside lamp down.'

Rose lifted the lamp down and shone it under the bed. Joshua stayed there for a few moments and then slid out. He shook his head.

'It looks untouched. No cuts in the floorboards. Nothing.'

Rose replaced the bedside light. On the cabinet she saw an envelope. On the front of it were the words *Last Will and Testament* in a strong black font. Written in handwriting underneath was *Stuart Johnson*. Rose picked it up. She hadn't seen it there earlier when she'd been unpacking the box.

'I found his will in this drawer. It wasn't even with all his proper paperwork,' Joshua said.

'You tried the loft and the garage?' Skeggsie said.

Joshua nodded glumly.

'It has to be somewhere that you would never go,' Skeggsie said.

'There's just one other place.'

'Where?'

'The MG!'

'What?'

'The car that Stu has been renovating for the last five

years. It was the one thing he got stroppy with me about. *Don't ever touch it*, he said. *It's my pride and joy.'*

Joshua was out of the room and off down the stairs. He went into the kitchen and through the door that linked the house with the garage. Rose was behind him. Poppy forced her way through. Skeggsie followed. The garage was freezing. In the middle of it sat a car covered with tarpaulin. Rose hugged herself while Joshua began to fiddle with ropes and ties. After a few minutes' exertion he pulled the tarpaulin off the sports car. He stood back, the rubberised covering falling about him on the ground. Rose wondered whether she should gather it up.

'I don't know where it could be. It's not exactly big, is it?'

It was a two-seater car. Most of it was blue but one wing was a dark grey. It had no tyres and was up on blocks. Joshua opened the door and pushed the seats forward.

'There's barely enough room for two people to sit in here,' he said.

He went to the back of the car and opened the boot. There was a spare tyre screwed down. He looked round the garage and then stepped across and picked up a spanner. He began to loosen the wheel nut, grunting several times until it came off.

'Hold that,' he said, giving Rose the nut and spanner.

He pulled the wheel off but there was nothing underneath. He stood still one hand pushing his hair back.

'Has this car ever been driven?' Skeggsie said.

He shook his head. He was clearly upset.

'What about there?' he said, pointing at the bonnet.

'The engine?'

'Maybe he was rebuilding that as well.'

Joshua didn't answer. He looked perturbed and walked round to the front of the car and fiddled with something. There was a click and the bonnet came up. He pulled out a rod and fitted it into the bodywork and the bonnet stayed up.

'Well, well . . .'

Rose looked in. There were some sections of engine, oily and black. On the right-hand side there was something covered with a tea towel. Joshua took it out and let the towel drop. It was a steel box like the one they had in the kitchen. This one was the size of a ring binder, slim and locked. Without a word Joshua walked back to the kitchen, Rose and Skeggsie following him, closing the cold of the garage out. He placed the box on the table. Skeggsie picked up the key and opened the box.

Inside was a pile of newspaper clippings. Joshua took them out.

Underneath was a notebook. The three of them stared at it.

It was exactly the same type as the two they already had. Skeggsie picked it up and placed it on the table, carefully as though it might break. Then he opened the first page. There, just like the other two books, was a photograph. This time it wasn't a man, or a teenage boy. It was a young girl wearing a school uniform and smiling at the camera. Underneath was handwriting, five words printed out in sturdy capitals.

JUDY GREAVES THE BUTTERFLY MURDER

TWELVE

'The Butterfly Murder?' Rose said. 'What is *that*?'

'I don't know,' Joshua said, pulling the book from her.

Skeggsie was looking closely at the pile of newspaper clippings. In among them was a folded large brown envelope that had been roughly opened. Rose looked at it all with mounting frustration. What did this have to do with anything else? They didn't need more information. They needed to make some sense of the information they already had.

'There's no code in this book. Look at the first page. It's handwritten. It's Stu's handwriting. Then it's just newspaper stories. Stuck in, page after page.'

'Let's see. Put it here on the table so that we can all read it,' said Skeggsie.

Joshua flattened the book on to the surface of the table. The three of them stood very still, reading the text that was in front of them.

The Butterfly Murder

June 2002. Ten-year-old Judy Greaves went missing. She was in a car in a supermarket car park with her older sister. Her sister got out of the car at one point to go and remind the mother to buy something. When she returned the car was empty.

The sister hadn't been able to find the mother and was now afraid of being in trouble. So she did nothing until the mother came back. At first she told the mother that Judy had gone into the shop to find her. The mother ran back into the shop and looked everywhere. She went back to the car and still there was no sign of her. She alerted the staff. The police were called and the area scoured. No one in the car park saw anything. A nearby CCTV camera picked up an image of a black Ford Explorer leaving the area soon after. There was a man in the driving seat and a girl in the passenger seat.

There was no other sighting of interest.

Five days later a body was discovered in a room in an empty house, 6 Primrose Crescent. The house belonged to an elderly man who had gone into care. The girl was found by an estate agent who had come to meet a client. The room was unfurnished except for pictures on the wall of mounted butterflies. The walls were covered in these pictures as though someone had been a serious collector. The crime became known as the Butterfly Murder.

After a thorough examination human DNA was obtained from hair fibres that were found on the floor of the room. Those fibres belonged to thirty-eight-year-old Simon Lister, a painter and decorator from Newcastle who had a criminal record for abuse of a minor. He also ran a dark blue Ford Explorer.

He was charged with the murder of Judy Greaves. The trial look place almost a year to the day that she went missing.

At the trial Simon Lister's defence was that six months previously he had decorated that room for the owner, Mr Timothy Lucas, before he was taken into care. His barrister made the case that in an empty, unused house hair fibres could lie for a long time.

Simon Lister was acquitted.

Joshua checked that they'd all read it and then he turned the pages of the notebook. The newspaper clippings were in date order. The headlines read like a narrative. **Ten-Year-Old Girl Abducted from Morrisons' Car Park; Please Give Us Our Daughter Back, Mother Pleads; CCTV Footage Used to Identify Car; Black Ford Involved in Snatch of Girl: Mother Makes Second Plea; Re-enactment of Abduction in Morrisons' Car Park; Child's Body Discovered in Empty**

House; Room of Death Wallpapered in Butterflies; The Butterfly Collector; Girl Found Dead Among Specimens; Six Hundred Attend Butterfly Girl Funeral; 38-Year-Old Man Arrested For Butterfly Girl; DNA Evidence Will Pin Down Butterfly Murder; Butterfly Murder Trial Begins; Judy Held For Days Before Murder; Trial Halted As Family Members Abuse Accused; Butterfly Jury Out; Not Guilty of Judy's Murder; Butterfly Accused Found Not Guilty.

Joshua turned the pages. After that the lined pages were empty.

'This letter,' Skeggsie said, as he flattened it on to the table.

'It's Dad's writing.'

The letter was dated 18th May, 2004. The handwriting was neat, slanted, sometimes difficult to read.

Dear Stu,

Thanks for sending me the information about this terrible case. I've returned the scrapbook you sent. I hadn't realised it happened in Primrose Crescent, so close to you. The details are shocking. I'd read about it in the national papers of course – who could forget the Butterfly Murder – and of course the terrible business of the killer getting off. Getting away with murder is not a new thing but it's particularly upsetting when it concerns a child. I expect the police in Newcastle have Simon Lister in their sights.

My new job is working on cold cases and you're right
that these are old unsolved crimes. Most of the stuff I
look into is to do with organised crime. You wouldn't
believe how many so-called respectable people get
away with murder (and worse) by organising other
people to do their dirty work for them. So my
colleagues and I spend months on a particular
network, say drugs or trafficking, and sometimes we
have success and sometimes we achieve nothing.
What I'm going to say here is harsh. The murder of a
ten-year-old girl does not fit into the cold cases brief.
Especially as it seems clear that they know who the
murderer is but simply don't have the evidence. It's
really up to the local force to continue investigating
it. My boss has his 'targets' and this case is not
among them. Really sorry.

I know you said that the girl's sister is in your form
group at school. Dreadful for her but lucky she's got
you as her teacher. You'll look after her, I know you
will.

Josh is well and I've met this new woman, Kathy.
She's just been transferred to our team. She's pretty
amazing and I think things might work out for us.
She's got a daughter, Rose, who plays the violin.

I was thinking of coming up to see you in August,
maybe the weekend of the 23rd. Kathy and I could
drive up on Friday night and come back Monday. Her

daughter can stay with a friend and so can Josh. It's
ages since I saw you and I'd like you to meet her!
Sorry again about not being able to help regarding
the Butterfly Murder. Bren

The three of them were quiet. Skeggsie had turned away and was looking at the remaining cuttings which he'd spread over the table. He seemed to be sorting them out into some order. Rose read over the letter again. Joshua was muttering.

'Stu must have asked Dad to take on this case. This girl who was murdered. He must have sent this book of clippings to Dad and then Dad said he couldn't.'

Skeggsie was moving the clippings around on the table.

'Why aren't they in the book?' Rose said, pointing.

'These date from *after* your dad's reply.'

Joshua closed the book and Rose moved round the table so that she was on the other side of Skeggsie. She scanned the headlines. **Man Accused of Butterfly Murder Found Dead; Butterfly Case Man Slain; Accused Man Died From Single Stab Wound; Lister Found Dead in Front Garden; Simon Lister Killed in Cold Blood.**

'He was killed on Saturday 23rd August,' Skeggsie said. 'Someone knocked on his door and he went to answer it. He was stabbed once in the heart and his body pulled behind a hedge in his front garden. He was found by the next-door neighbour the following morning.'

'Twenty-third of August, the weekend that Dad said he might come up. What do we do with all this?' Joshua said, sighing. 'What does it mean?'

'Got your laptop?' Skeggsie asked.

Rose nodded. She went upstairs and picked it up off her bed and turned it on as she walked back down. She placed it on the table. Skeggsie sat down and tapped the keyboard. After a few moments he let out a low whistle.

'Look at this!'

He spun the laptop round and on the screen Rose saw a single newspaper story. It was big, perhaps from a front page.

Butterfly Killer Had Planned Another Murder

The killing of Simon Lister two weeks ago has prevented a second murder. Police sources say that searches of Lister's house and his computer have shown details of a second child who he had been stalking. His computer showed hundreds of pictures of the girl who the police are calling Child X. Along with this are lurid plans to abduct and murder this girl. Police have also found evidence of a lock-up which was hitherto unknown. In this lock-up there were items of Judy Greaves's clothes which were not found at the time her body was discovered. They have also found, disturbingly, items of clothing belonging to at least two other unnamed girls.

An inquiry is being set up to investigate these items and the identity of the victims of this sexual predator.

Police say that the hunt for the murderer of Simon Lister is ongoing.

Skeggsie clicked on a couple more articles. The headlines were the same: Butterfly Killer Proven at Last; Justice at Last for Judy's Killer; Butterfly Murderer a Serial Killer?; Simon Lister's Murder Saves Second Girl.

Joshua had sat down. Rose was the only one standing. She felt agitated by what she'd read. She felt like she wanted to walk up and down. The three of them were frowning, Skeggsie with a small V in his forehead, Joshua with his eyebrows pursed, Rose chewing her lip.

Eventually Skeggsie spoke.

'Do you think Stu might have done this?'

Joshua shook his head fiercely. 'Stabbed Simon Lister? No! Stu is such a gentle guy. You know him, Skeggs. You know he wouldn't hurt a fly!'

Skeggsie nodded. He caught Rose's eye and gave a slight shrug.

'Why did he keep all this stuff?' Rose said.

'Because it meant something to him? Because he felt for this girl in his class, the sister of the dead girl?'

'Why keep it locked up? And then there's the notebook . . .'

'It's an exercise book, Rose. School is full of them. There's no code in it. It's probably got nothing to do with the others. This is just something that Stu kept for reasons of his own. I'm going to put it away now,' he said.

He stood up, opened the steel box, scooped up the clippings and the book and the envelope and tossed them back inside. Then he slammed the lid down and locked it.

'Then there's the name, *butterfly*,' Rose said, glancing down at her arm where her tattoo was.

'Stu did not have a tattoo of a butterfly. He did not!'

'Don't get upset,' Rose said.

'How can I not get upset! My uncle would never do anything like that. He just couldn't. He is a good person.'

'I'll do some research at Dad's, ask him about this case. He was in post then. There's bound to be something he remembers about it.'

Joshua nodded stiffly.

'Let's go to the pub tonight,' Skeggsie said. 'It's Christmas Eve. We'll have a drink at the Lighthouse. Let's just leave all this stuff to ferment for a while.'

Joshua got up without answering. He went out of the room with the steel box under his arm. They heard him go up the stairs.

'This is complicated,' Skeggsie said.

'I'll try to get him out tonight.'

'I bet I'll find something about this on the net,

something more telling than the newspapers. And I'll call Eddie about the registration number of the SUV.'

She walked to the door. Outside the snow was falling heavily, making a white carpet on the pathway. Skeggsie put his hood up.

'Thanks for coming round,' Rose said.

'No thanks needed.'

She watched him walk and remembered his new haircut. Just like Eddie's.

THIRTEEN

When Joshua returned from the hospital Rose hovered around him. She was anxious, wondering how he'd got on with his uncle after the discovery of the phone and the Butterfly Murder papers.

'I never said anything to Stu about what we found,' he said. 'He seems much better now. His MRI scan was clear and they're talking about discharging him in two or three days.'

'That's good,' she said. 'I'll come with you tomorrow to see him.'

He nodded.

'I can't talk to him about any of this, Rose. It's all too mixed up in my head. It's like there's this other person emerging from my uncle, a guy I thought I knew really well. But still, why should that surprise me? I thought I knew my dad well.'

Rose nodded. People weren't always the way they seemed.

Then he'd gone upstairs and had been in Stuart's bedroom most of the afternoon. There was no banging of drawers or sounds of anything being moved around so she guessed that he was sitting at Stu's computer, opening and closing files, looking through Stu's search history, trying to find clues as to what had been going on in his uncle's life.

Rose turned the television off. The place was untidy but she couldn't be bothered with it. She made two hot drinks, a tea for her and a milky coffee for Joshua. She took them upstairs and pushed Stuart's bedroom door open. The room was in a mess, the bed still moved out of its place from when they had been searching earlier. Joshua was staring at the computer screen. To the side of the keyboard she could see the cream envelope with the words *Last Will and Testament. Stuart Johnson.*

'Hi,' she said. 'Here's a drink.'

'Thanks.'

'I'm going to meet Skeggsie at the pub tonight,' she said. 'Why don't you come?'

'I need to get this stuff out of the way first.'

She put her drink down and laid her hand on his shoulder. 'Just come for a couple of hours – to give us a break. Then we can start thinking straight about all this.'

He placed his hand over hers. 'I don't know what I'd do if it wasn't for you, Rosie,' he said, his voice croaky.

'Don't say . . .'

She couldn't continue. His hand was holding on to hers tightly.

'I can be a real pain but . . .'

He was staring into the screen and couldn't see her face. She was glad. Her feelings were probably written all over it. She ruffled the back of his head with her other hand, his hair wiry in her fingers.

'And Skeggsie,' she said. 'Don't forget him.'

He turned round, letting her hand go.

'Of course. Skeggsie is crucial. I just wish you two liked each other more.'

'We're getting there,' she said.

About nine she changed her clothes to go out. She wore a black blouse and jeans. She got her tiny make-up bag out and applied eyeshadow, thick mascara and plum lipstick, then put on the blue earrings. Two shining discs of colour that contrasted with her smoky eyes and dark pink lips.

Why not? It was Christmas Eve.

Joshua came out into the hall as she was going.

'You look different,' he said.

She was looking in the hall mirror, pulling her coat on, getting ready to leave.

'It's the earrings,' she said, opening the front door. 'They give me that bit of sparkle. See you later?'

She stepped out into the snow, pulling her hood up.

'In an hour or so,' he called after her.

Walking along the dark streets towards the Promenade she wondered if he would come. The snow crunched under her feet and some cold air seemed to worm its way up her sleeves. She hugged herself and walked more quickly. She turned out of the street and on to the road that led up to the Promenade.

It was dark, a couple of the streetlights not working. She speeded up and almost bumped into a man as he stepped out of a shop doorway.

'*Big Issue*?' he said, holding a magazine inside a plastic wrapper.

'You made me jump!' she said angrily.

'Sorry, missus,' he said.

She stepped round him and walked on but then felt bad. When she looked back he'd retreated into the doorway. She made a tsking sound and got some coins out of her purse. Then she paused. She pulled a note out. It would leave her a bit short but she could probably find a machine somewhere tomorrow or the next day. She walked back to the doorway and held out the note.

'Thank you, missus,' the man said and held out a copy of the magazine but she waved it away and walked on, holding the sides of her hood so that it didn't blow back.

The pub was busy. Skeggsie was already there in the back room, saving some seats. Rose edged her way up to the bar. A weary-looking woman served her, calling her 'pet' four times. She bought two bottles of beer and then struggled through the crowd to get to the back room. It was less crowded there and the music was lower.

'Here you are,' she said.

'Thanks.'

'Did you get a chance to talk to your dad?'

He nodded. 'He knew loads about it. In 2002, when the murder happened, he was attached to the Wallsend district. The murder was in the Whitley Bay area so he didn't deal with it directly but everyone knew about it and some of the detectives in Wallsend were transferred across to take part in the investigation. He said it was talked about for months.'

'You didn't mention Stuart?'

''Course not! I'm not an idiot.'

'Sorry.'

'Dad said that the police in Whitley Bay were certain that Simon Lister was the killer. They were furious when he was acquitted. For months afterwards they kept an unofficial eye on him but he never put a foot wrong. When he was murdered a cheer went up in the pub that the police used. They had to maintain a professional stance of course but then they found things that were chilling. He was a very nasty man, my dad said.'

'They never solved the crime.'

'They tried to. They had to. It was all over the papers and it had to look as though they were trying. They investigated two of the jurors and the lead detectives on the case. They interviewed over a hundred people. Simon Lister had a lot of enemies but they didn't find any evidence. In the end a policeman from London was brought in to look at the case.'

Rose drank her beer.

'My dad said that the feeling among the ordinary detectives was that whoever stabbed Simon Lister deserved an award, not a prison sentence. Whoever did it actually saved the life of another girl who Lister was planning to abduct.'

'But whoever did it didn't know that at the time. That wasn't known until after.'

'True but isn't the world a better place without someone like Lister in it?'

Rose frowned. 'You can't believe that? That murder is right?'

'Maybe in this case it was.'

'But murder is *never* right.'

Skeggsie shrugged. Rose was about to argue with him when she saw Rory Spenser come into the room. He stopped at the doorway and looked round. When he saw Skeggsie he stared for a moment, stony-faced. Then he gave a cold smile. Rose did not like him at all.

'That's all I need. Him in my face,' Skeggsie said.

'Just ignore him,' she said.

'I tried ignoring him when I was at school. It left me covered in bruises.'

She didn't answer. Rory Spenser walked over to a slot machine and began to play. She felt Skeggsie relax.

'What have you found out about the SUV?' she said.

'Eddie has traced it to a company called Beaufort Holdings. They're based in Chelsea.'

'Not far from South Kensington,' she said, thinking of the restaurant owned by Lev Baranski.

'I'm going to go on to the Companies House website and see what I can find out about them.'

'Thanks for doing it, Skeggs.'

Just then Rory Spenser left the room without looking at them. It made her feel better. Maybe he would go off to another pub. She'd passed a couple on her way there, the music blaring, smokers standing on the pavement huddled together for warmth.

'What time did Josh say he'd get here?'

'Any time soon.'

The conversation about the Simon Lister murder had made her feel uneasy. It would have to be spoken about again when Joshua got here, or certainly tomorrow at Skeggsie's, probably over Christmas dinner. Skeggsie's dad would no doubt delight in having a tale to tell, unaware of the information they had found in Stuart's belongings.

She drank her beer, feeling the cold fizz in her mouth. She shrugged her coat off and pushed it to the back of her seat. She'd been freezing outside but the pub was hot and loud and the snow seemed far away.

'I might play darts. There's a kid over there I know,' Skeggsie said.

'You go on. I'll save the seats.'

As Skeggsie walked away she saw Martin come into the room. He looked around for a minute then noticed her and walked in her direction.

'All right?' he said, smiling.

She nodded and moved along the seat so that he could sit down. He looked her up and down.

'You look nice,' he said.

He was wearing a polo shirt and some jeans.

'You look nice too.'

'Boys don't look *nice*. They look cool or smart or fit.'

'Take the compliment as it comes,' she said.

'You're a hard girl.'

'Just straight. Aren't you cold?'

'This is Newcastle. We don't wear coats in the winter,' he said.

'Really?'

'Joking. My duffle's in the other bar with some of my mates.'

The music got louder all of a sudden.

'You didn't come for a drink the other night.'

'I didn't say I would.'

'You broke my heart.'

She smiled and shook her head.

'You know what I think?' he said in her ear.

She shook her head.

'I think you're carrying a torch for someone.'

She looked at him straight in the eye. Was she that easy to read?

'I think your *heart* is elsewhere.'

'Just because I didn't go out with you? Might it be because I'm not attracted to you?'

'You know how to hurt a guy. No. It can't be that. Every girl is attracted to me.'

'It must be your modesty that wins them over!'

'I'll see you later,' he said, grabbing her hand and squeezing it in a friendly way.

She looked across to the dartboard for Skeggsie and was taken aback to see Joshua standing next to him, staring at her. She raised her hand but lowered it again because his face was flat, unreadable. He turned his back and talked with Skeggsie and she felt as though he'd blocked her out, as though he was angry with her for some reason. She should get up and go over and speak to him but she was afraid she would lose the seats. She had to sit there, uneasy as Skeggsie and Joshua talked. After a few minutes she couldn't stand it any more. She got up and marched across the room.

'What's up?' she said.

'Joshua's found something.'

'What? Why didn't you come over and tell me?'

'I thought you looked busy, Rosie,' Joshua said.

'I was just chatting with . . .'

'You looked like you were enjoying yourself.'

'I was . . . I'm sorry. Am I supposed to walk round with a miserable face all the time?'

'Never mind. Look, I found something important,' Joshua said. 'I'm going to show it to Skeggs outside. Come if you want.'

' 'Course I want to come,' she said.

Joshua and Skeggsie walked away towards the back door where the smokers' garden was. Wearily, not sure exactly what it was she'd done wrong, Rose followed them.

FOURTEEN

The night air was speckled with snow in the smokers' area. The small courtyard was lit up by Christmas lights that were strung from corner to corner. In the middle was a patio heater. Several people were huddled up to it, cigarettes perched in gloved hands. Moments after Rose stepped outside she realised that she'd left her coat on the chair in the pub. She half turned to go and get it but Joshua was looking agitated.

'What have you found?' she said, rubbing her hands together to warm them up.

He shoved an envelope at her. It had some writing on the front and had been opened.

'I found this inside my uncle's Last Will and Testament.'

'You opened it?'

'It was the only thing I hadn't searched.'

Just then the pub door opened and Rory Spenser came out. Rose felt Joshua stiffen at the sight of him. The smokers standing round the fire stopped talking and called out to him. Rory Spenser had a cigarette in his hand and a lighter which he was pumping without success.

'Look who's here. The boy Skeggs and his minder. You do know that this is a smoking area, right? For grown-ups, I mean.'

Joshua swore at Rory. A flame jumped from the lighter and Rory fed it to the cigarette. He inhaled deeply then blew out a stream of smoke towards Skeggsie.

'You're all words these days, Johnson. Has London softened you?'

'Give it a rest, Spenser,' Skeggsie said, turning to him.

Rory grinned at him.

'You get some bottle from down in London, *Darren*?'

'He's giving me a headache,' Skeggsie said and turned back to Joshua.

'Go and smoke somewhere else, Spenser,' Joshua said, stepping out in front of him.

'It's all right . . .' Skeggsie said.

'I don't want you here,' Joshua said, moving towards Rory Spenser.

'What? You going to hit me? Like you did before?'

'If I have to.'

'Don't, Josh . . . He's entitled to come out . . .' Skeggsie said, pulling Joshua away from Rory.

'Do what you're told, Joshua,' Rory said, a smile on his face.

Skeggsie turned and stared at Rory for a few seconds. Then he seemed to lurch towards him and push him away so that Rory stumbled backwards and fell against the wall. Skeggsie stood over him and Rose could see his fists clenched as if he was waiting for the other boy to get up and hit him. The other smokers crowded round and Rose found herself being edged here and there. Then the pub door opened and Martin came out. He looked around and saw what had happened. He pushed Skeggsie away and told the other smokers to back off. He helped Rory up to his feet.

'Been training in London, Darren?' Rory said, still smirking.

'Leave it,' Martin said. 'Go back in the pub.'

Rory brushed himself down.

'I want a smoke!'

'Go and do it somewhere else,' Joshua said.

Rory shrugged and stood his ground. The other smokers wandered back to the heater. A couple went off into the street beyond. Martin was looking puzzled.

'You let him wind you up?' he said to Joshua.

'He's scum. He was like it at school and he's like it now. I don't know what sort of crusade you think you're on, Marty, but it's a waste of time. He's just like his brother.'

'You should cool it, Josh,' Martin said, putting a hand on Joshua's shoulder, his voice low and placatory.

Joshua shook it off.

Rose looked at him with dismay. Joshua was so *angry* all the time. To her he always seemed soft and easy-going and wouldn't hurt a fly. Up here, in Newcastle, he was like a lit firework, ready to go off. Skeggsie was standing beside him looking upset, his shoulders rounded.

'You can't keep doing this,' he hissed. 'You have to let me fight my own battles, mate!'

'Fine. You do it! I thought I was helping.'

'You have. You did. But now you have to stop. I'm a man now. You have to let me do it.'

'A *man*, that's a laugh,' Rory called.

'Shut up, Spenser,' Martin shouted. 'What did I tell you about that big mouth of yours?'

'Get him out of my sight,' Joshua said.

Martin exhaled. Some of the other smokers took Rory back into the pub and Martin followed. Rose watched them go and felt her shoulders loosen. She registered the envelope in her hand that Joshua had given her. She tried to smooth it out but her fingers were trembling with the cold.

'Why does Rory hate you so?' she said to Skeggsie.

'My dad locked his brother up years ago.'

'Oh.'

The three of them were on their own in the courtyard. It seemed bleaker now, the colours jaded. The snow was slanting down. To Rose it felt like tiny grains of ice pricking her skin. She stepped sideways towards the door. Her fingers were so cold they were hurting.

'I'm going into the pub. I'm freezing,' Rose said. 'Are you coming?'

'What about the letter? Can't you even be bothered to read it?' Joshua said, his face like thunder.

'Why are you so furious at me? At everyone?'

'Read it.'

Frowning, she looked at the envelope. On it were the words *Only to be opened by Charles Jensen.*

'Who's Charles Jensen?'

'Stu's solicitor.'

She took out a piece of paper that had been folded in half. Across it were two sentences and a signature.

I alone am guilty of the murder of Simon Lister. I take full responsibility and I have no regrets. Stuart Robert Johnson

She read it twice to be sure of what it was saying.

'Oh no!'

'What do I do with that?' Joshua said.

Rose passed it to Skeggsie. He read it.

'You were right and I was wrong. My uncle really is a killer.'

'No, it doesn't say that exactly . . .'

'Go on, say I told you so! Say it!'

'Josh . . .'

She reached out her hand to him.

'It's Christmas Eve. We can't do anything about this now. Come into the warm. We can think about all this the day after tomorrow.'

But Joshua was still railing.

'You think I can just postpone the way I'm feeling, Rosie? Just file this away again and not think about it? What happens when I face my uncle tomorrow? What do I say to him when I know that he's written this? After everything else that I've lost it seems like I've lost him as well. He's not the person I thought he was . . .'

'This will be sorted . . .' Skeggsie said.

'How can you know that? You don't understand.'

'What's that supposed to mean?' Skeggsie said.

'I mean you haven't been in the same situation as me and Rose.'

'Because of your parents?'

Joshua nodded.

'I lost my mother when I was ten,' Skeggsie said angrily. 'She didn't disappear. She just lay in a bed and faded away. I watched her every day for months and then one day she was dead.'

Skeggsie held out the envelope to Joshua.

'I didn't mean that . . .'

'Yes, you did. The last couple of months it's all you ever talk about. Her and you. Your dad, her mum.'

'But you've helped . . .'

''Course I have. But sometimes it's like you two are the only people in the world who've ever felt loss. You're not the only ones who have a right to be angry with the world.'

Skeggsie walked away into the pub. The door closed and then it was just the two of them.

Joshua looked at Rose. His eyes had glassed over.

'I should go home.'

'No, don't,' she said, holding her hand out to him.

'I've messed it up. I can't stay here.'

He turned and strode away from the festive lights and into the darkness of the street beyond.

Rose, her jaw trembling with cold, was left standing on her own.

FIFTEEN

Rose went back into the pub. She stood for a few minutes soaking up the heat. The room was packed and she made herself breathe slowly as people brushed by her holding trays of drinks. She looked back to the door and wondered whether Joshua had really gone home or whether he might burst in again and then everything would be all right. The row, the bad feeling, the letter written by Stuart – maybe these things could be set aside for one night and they could just be together in the warmth of the pub for a couple of hours on Christmas Eve. She looked round. Rory Spencer wasn't in the room but Skeggsie was – over by the dartboard, standing by himself, watching a couple of people play.

She walked across to him.

'Sorry, Skeggs,' she said. 'Me and Josh have been preoccupied. We don't always think things through.'

'No, you don't.'

'There's a lot going on at the moment.'

'You got any more clichés, Rose?'

Rose blew through her teeth. Why was talking to Skeggsie so difficult?

'I've got to be straight,' she said. 'You've never been my favourite person . . .'

'Are you trying to cheer me up?'

'You're too cold for me. You've got no social skills. What I'm trying to say is that, if I'm honest, I don't always like you very much. But I am *fond* of you.'

'That doesn't make any sense,' he said, a mocking expression on his face.

'It does,' Rose continued, ignoring him. 'Think about it. In any case what does it matter? Josh is your real friend. You've only ever put up with me because of him. And you know that he leans on you. God, he never stops talking about you.'

Skeggsie sighed. 'I know he's always fighting my battles.'

'He needs you now. He needs *us* now.'

Skeggsie nodded.

'On top of everything there's his uncle's *confession*.'

'I know.'

'How does Josh live with that?'

'I don't know.'

'Things just get worse.' Rose said.

'Where is he now?'

'He went home. He knows he's upset you.'

'I'll go after him.'

'You want me to come?'

Skeggsie shook his head. 'I need to have a talk with him. Sort this fighting stuff out once and for all. Then I'll bring him back here.'

'Will you mention the letter?'

'Not tonight. It's bad news for Josh but looking at it another way it's a development. Joshua is too upset to see that now but it's another step to finding out what happened to your parents.'

Rose felt bad at the mention of parents. Skeggsie had been right. It was the main thing they all talked about. Her and Josh's life. They hardly ever mentioned his. Maybe Joshua thought that fighting Skeggsie's battles was all he needed to do. It would have to change.

'Have you been in touch with Eddie?' she said, raising her voice so that he could hear.

'Been emailing.'

'What's he doing for Christmas?'

'He's staying with his sister. He doesn't get on with his parents.'

'Maybe when we get back to London he could come round.'

'I don't think so.'

'How come?'

'Him and me, we're into animation and other stuff. I don't want him sucked into what Josh and me do.'

'What about me? Don't I get to meet him?'

'I only introduce my friends to people who like me!'

'Right,' she said, smiling weakly at Skeggsie's attempt at a joke.

'I'd better go and sort things out with Josh. You waiting here?'

Rose hesitated. Actually she didn't want to stay in the pub any more but she sensed that it was better to let Skeggsie go and see Joshua alone.

'Yes, text me when you're on your way back and I'll get some drinks in.'

'OK.'

'Skeggs?' she said, pulling his arm just as he was walking off. 'I'm sorry. About your mum, I mean. I know you told me before she'd died but I had no idea it was such a tough time for you. No idea at all.'

'Yeah, well . . .'

Skeggsie gave her a stiff smile and walked off, sidestepping other drinkers. Rose leant back against the wall and wondered how long it would take him to get back to Joshua's, have a talk and bring him back to the pub. Thirty minutes? More like forty-five.

'Want to play darts, pet?' a voice said.

She turned and saw a thin man in a leather jacket. He had a moustache that curled up at each side.

'Go on then,' she said and took three darts from him.

*   *   *

After the game she walked across to the chairs where she'd originally been sitting to get her coat. The girls who were in the seats passed it across and she let it hang over her arm. Now she was too hot to wear it and she had nowhere to put it. She stood aimlessly. The back room was more crowded than before and she had to keep moving back and forth as people went past her. Even the dartboard had closed and the area was filling up with people. She walked across to the door and went through into the main bar where music was playing. It was loud, a wave of sound that washed over her. The bar had flashing lights and she could see a DJ on the tiny stage. There was a dance floor and several people were on it. She bought a beer and found a corner to stand in. Pulling her phone out, she saw that Skeggsie had been gone for over thirty minutes. They should be back soon or if Josh wasn't going to come then Skeggsie would text her – she was sure he would.

Martin saw her then. He was standing with a group of friends. They were talking and laughing. Looking more carefully she tried to see if Rory Spenser was there but he was not. Then she looked around the rest of the bar but there was no sign of him. Martin headed in her direction.

'I thought you'd gone,' he said. 'Come over to us.'

She shook her head.

'You look lonely over here.'

'Josh and Skeggs are coming. I'm waiting for them.'

'Sure?' he said, looking puzzled.

She nodded.

'Josh upset with me? About the Rory situation?'

'I don't know.'

'Joshua and me go back a long way. We'll be all right.'

'He's just upset about his uncle and other stuff.'

' 'Course he is. We all know that. Stuart is a really good guy. Well, I'll see you. Have a good Christmas.'

He turned and walked away and she moved towards the pub door to wait for Joshua and Skeggsie. It was cooler there so she put her coat on. The music wasn't so loud and she felt the tension drain out of her.

Then the door opened and Joshua walked in.

The shoulders of his big coat were covered in speckles of snow. She smiled, pleased to see him but puzzled that she hadn't received a text. Had Skeggsie simply forgotten her? Joshua walked over, grabbed her arm and squeezed it.

'Sorry, Rose. I've been a prat. I don't know what to say. I feel as if everything's . . .'

'It's OK. I'm sorry. Both me and Skeggsie were worried about you.'

'Anyway, you were right, there's nothing we can do about any of it now. We'll just have to talk it over tomorrow, after we get back from Skeggsie's Christmas dinner.'

Rose felt herself relax. It was the old Joshua again.

'I'll get a drink,' Joshua said. 'You ready for another? Where's Skeggs? Playing darts?'

'No, he went to get you. I thought he was with you. He said he was going to your house. About half an hour, forty minutes or so ago. I thought that was why you came.'

'No, I just cooled down,' Joshua said, getting his phone out. 'I'll ring him. See what he's up to.'

'I'll get the drinks.'

Rose stood at the bar until a young lad served her. She bought two beers and then took them over to Joshua who was looking at his mobile.

'No answer,' he said, shaking his head. 'Maybe he was just too peed off with me.'

'No, he was definitely going to get you. He was fine. I cheered him up,' she said.

'You *cheered* him up?'

'We get along,' she said, drinking her beer straight from the bottle.

'We'll give him ten minutes then send out a search party.'

'He'll probably turn up any minute.'

She stood by Joshua as more people came into the pub. It was no longer possible to see to the other side of the bar. Rose looked at her mobile. She wondered if Skeggsie had changed his mind. Had he walked out of the pub, gone in Joshua's direction, and begun to feel angry about the evening? Had he gone home instead, perhaps feeling thoroughly fed up with both of them? A feeling of guilt niggled at her. What had she said? *I don't always like you very much. But I am* fond *of you.* Why had she put it like that? Thinking about it now it seemed a pretty insensitive thing to say. Maybe Skeggsie had had enough and they'd have to wait and see if he was still friends with them tomorrow, Christmas Day, when they were meant to be having Christmas dinner with him and his dad.

'There's no answer from his mobile. You think he just went home?'

'I don't know.'

'Let's go round there. It's only ten minutes' walk. I don't really want to leave things as they are.'

'What if he went home to get something *then* went to your house? He might well be on his way here now. If we walk towards his house we might miss him altogether.'

'Good thinking. We'll go to his house via mine. Then we shouldn't miss him.'

Rose put her bottle down and pushed open the pub doors. The cold air hit her and she pulled her coat tight. It had begun snowing again. She could see it in the streetlights. They walked along in silence, coming up to a small group of people who were talking cheerfully. A couple of girls were linking arms and singing in harmony. It was a Christmas song that Rose liked. Behind them she noticed the homeless man that she'd seen earlier walking along towards her, holding his copy of the *Big Issue* in front of him. No doubt he was trying to drum up some money from the pub-goers.

They turned off the Promenade and into the side streets. They passed a fish and chip shop and there was the strong smell of frying. She was suddenly hungry and she realised that she was also feeling a little woozy. She'd had at least three beers on top of an empty stomach. It hadn't been the sort of day when she'd thought much about food. Maybe she could make some omelettes when they got in.

Joshua was looking at his phone again and she'd fallen behind him. They were in the darker part of the road, moving further away from the seafront. She quickened her step to catch up with him. They were walking alongside a row of shops, some of which were boarded up. A bus passed on the other side, its window lit up to show people moving along the aisle to get off at the seafront.

When it was gone the road was very quiet.

Joshua put his phone away.

She heard a noise.

'You all right?' he said.

'What's that?'

'What?'

'That sound.'

She listened hard but all she could hear were shouts from a distant pub or club, cheering voices. When they quietened she walked on and then heard it again. A call from somewhere.

'It's coming from over there,' she said, pulling at Joshua's sleeve.

There was an alley between two shops. She looked hard to see what was in the darkness. There was nothing moving.

'Probably some drunks.'

She heard it again. A voice.

'No, listen.'

She looked over to the alley. It definitely came from that direction.

'There,' she pointed.

'Rosie, it's just some kids boozing or smoking dope. Or maybe making out.'

'*Making out?* What are you, American?'

She wanted to smile but then it came again. This time it sounded like a moan. She left Joshua where he was and walked across and stood at the gap between the two shops. It was pitch black. She held her mobile up for some light.

'Who's there?' she called. 'Is everything all right?'

There was a croaking sound. She pressed her mobile and it lit the area up for a split second then it went dark again.

'Someone's down here. Maybe they're ill or hurt.'

'Rosie. Kids hang out down there. I used to. Don't get involved . . .'

'How can you not get involved if someone's hurt? You can't just walk by.'

Joshua huffed, walked round her and stepped into the alley.

'Anyone there?' he called.

There was a sound but it was lower, a wheezing noise.

'What is it?' Rose said.

Joshua walked on a few steps. The darkness swallowed him up.

'Oh my God.'

'What?'

'Oh no.'

She followed Joshua into the alleyway. Her foot hit something and there was a sound of some animal scuttling away.

'What's happened?' she said, trying to see in the dark.

Joshua was kneeling on the ground, bending over.

'Skeggs.'

'What? Skeggsie? Is he all right? What's happened?'

'Skeggs, mate, where are you hurt?'

'What's happening? I can't see anything.'

'Have you been in a fight? Skeggs, what's happened to you?'

Rose stood very still, trying to peer over Joshua's shoulder. She pressed the buttons of her phone and caught a momentary view of Skeggsie's face. His head was flat on the ground and he looked as though he'd lost consciousness.

'Get an ambulance,' Joshua said, his voice breaking. 'Get an ambulance.'

'Right,' Rose said. 'I can't see in here. I'll go out into the street. Tell Skeggs they won't be long.'

The street was deserted when Rose pushed the buttons for 999. It rang for a few moments and she stamped her feet with impatience, all the while thinking about Skeggsie and what had happened. The face of Rory Spenser came into her head. When she spoke to the operator she was careful, enunciating her words, explaining what she thought had happened.

'My friend's hurt. I think there might have been a fight. He's passed out. We're in Jesmond Road by some shops and an alley. We're about five minutes' walk from the seafront.'

The woman's voice was calm, asking for details.

'I don't know how badly he's hurt,' she said. 'My other friend's helping him now. He might have concussion or something because he's not really moving.'

The woman continued asking questions.

'I'm not sure. The alley's dark so I couldn't see much,' Rose said. 'My friend's with him. How long do you think you'll be?'

The woman kept talking but Rose stopped listening to her.

Her eyes were fixed on Joshua who had come out of the alleyway. He was on his own.

'Josh?' she said.

He was in a mess. He stood under the streetlight and Rose could see a dark circle on his coat. It was a stain that had spread across the middle of it, raw and ugly. When she realised what it was she felt her throat tighten. In the back of her head she could hear a siren and then a burst of laughter from a nearby pub or club.

Her hands dropped to her side. The phone hung there.

'Is Skeggsie . . .' she said stupidly.

Joshua shook his head.

The blood looked oily, as if it might spread further. Joshua crossed his arms over it as if to staunch it. A blue light flashed on and off as the ambulance turned the corner and headed towards them.

SIXTEEN

Rose sat in the Accident and Emergency department. She watched what was going on in a kind of daze. People came in ones and twos, sometimes a group, sometimes accompanied by a police officer. They walked, limped or stumbled past a giant Christmas tree glittering with fairy lights. Underneath was an array of brightly wrapped boxes like some metallic island. They were greeted by nurses with bits of tinsel on their collars. There were smiles and calls of 'Merry Christmas'. In the background she thought she could hear some piped music – *Oh come, all ye faithful, joyful and triumphant!*

She gazed at these things as if she was watching a film.

Just then Bob Skeggs came in and rushed through the waiting area. He swept past and jumped into a lift just as the doors shut. She hardly registered who it was before he was gone. Beside her Joshua was stony. He was leaning forward in his seat, his elbows on his knees, staring down at the floor. He was an arm's length away from her but he might as well have been across the waiting room. He hadn't noticed Bob Skeggs. Maybe that was a good thing.

Skeggsie was gone.

The thought was dark and heavy and made her breathe fast and shallowly. She glanced sideways at Joshua. His shoulders were bent with the enormity of what had happened. His coat was heavy with Skeggsie's blood. His eyes were shut as though he only wanted darkness. He was in a world of his own.

'You think the doctors could have helped him?' Rose whispered.

'Rosie,' Joshua said, 'it's no good. He's . . .'

The word he wouldn't say. *Dead. Earth to earth, ashes to ashes*. She wished she was religious. She felt the need for a prayer, some kind of mantra that she could say to fill up the awful panic in her chest. She put her hand out sideways towards Joshua. She touched his coat and then felt his hand over hers. His skin felt cold and dry. From the piped music she could hear a familiar tune. *Silent night, holy night . . .*

Upstairs in a ward was Joshua's uncle. Tomorrow they were meant to visit him just like they were meant to have Christmas dinner at Skeggsie's house. But Rose knew these things wouldn't happen because their world had split apart.

Earlier, at the alley, there had been drama when the paramedics came. Joshua told them that Skeggsie was dead but still they got into action as though he hadn't spoken. They asked Joshua and Rose to move back, so that they had room to work. Then they began to try and resuscitate him. There were soft words that Rose could barely hear. They called him Darren because Joshua had told them his full name. Rose wanted to call out to them *He answers to Skeggsie* as if that was the only reason he wasn't responding.

A policeman turned up dropped off by a car with a siren. When he got out the car sped off somewhere else. He looked as young as they were and even though he had gloves on he was clenching his hands with the cold. He came up and asked them what had happened. Rose tried to explain how she'd heard a sound from the alley. At that moment the paramedics burst out of it, carrying Skeggsie on a stretcher towards the ambulance.

It gave Rose a moment's hope. They wouldn't take him to hospital unless they thought they could save him? The policeman walked over to them and had a brief conversation. Coming back, he shook his head and said, 'It doesn't look good.'

Joshua wanted to go in the ambulance but the paramedics told him to follow along. The young policeman pointed to the cab firm further up the street. Then he answered his mobile phone and began talking to someone. He walked away from them, his voice sombre. Rose was about to head towards the cab office but Joshua turned away from her and went back into the alley. The policeman had his back to him and didn't notice. Rose wondered what Joshua was doing. She stamped her feet on the ground, aware that the ambulance was getting further and further away.

Joshua reappeared, coming swiftly towards her. He had his hands in his pockets and only then did the young policeman look around. Rose followed him towards the cab office. There were people waiting outside smoking. Joshua went up to the counter and faced an elderly woman who had red hair tied up in a knot and Christmas tree earrings.

'My friend's been attacked and taken to hospital. He's . . . I know there's a queue but we need to get there quickly,' Joshua said, holding his voice steady.

'Eric's just come in, pet. The white Ford outside. I'll say a prayer for him.'

They got in the cab and as it raced off Joshua took something out of his pocket. Rose looked down at his hands.

Skeggsie's glasses. He'd picked them up from the alley.

They left the hospital just after three in the morning. A night bus took them part of the way back and they walked the rest. The streets were quiet. It was bitterly cold. Rose's breath came out in puffs and she could hear her feet crunching snow on the pavement. It was inky dark, no moon, the streetlights giving off a honeyed glow above them. The silence was broken from time to time by a distant laugh or an angry shout or a car accelerating along a nearby street.

Once indoors Joshua headed for the stairs, ignoring Poppy who was jumping up and down. Rose watched him disappear up to his room and close the door. She didn't know what to do. She had no energy to go after him because there was nothing she could say. Poppy was running around and Rose trudged to the back door to let her out into the garden. She looked round. The kitchen was a mess and there was a new whisky bottle opened, some of it already drunk. When the dog came back in she went into the living room. It was cold, the heating having gone off hours before. Her duvet was still there from where she'd brought it down that morning. Without taking her coat off she sat down on the sofa and lifted her feet up. She covered herself with the duvet and lay down, the dog on the carpet beside her.

When she woke up it was daylight and Joshua was looking down at her.

'Wake up, Rosie.'

She sat up too quickly. She was stiff from sleeping on the sofa and her coat was twisted under her. She looked at the clock. It was past ten. She'd slept for ages. Still, though, she felt dazed as if she'd only had a nap. The previous evening came back to her in a flash and she hugged the duvet.

'I'm going back to the alley,' Joshua said.

He was wearing his stained coat. The blood was rust coloured, darker in the middle, like a wound – a mirror image of Skeggsie.

'I'll come,' she said, averting her eyes. She forced herself to stand up and gathered the duvet together. 'Give me five minutes.'

She ran upstairs and used the toilet then splashed water on her face. Before leaving the bathroom she glanced in the mirror. There were dark circles under her eyes where the previous evening's make-up had smudged and run. She used some tissue to wipe it clean. She ran her fingers through her hair and went downstairs. Joshua was standing by the front door, jangling his keys. They walked out of the house into a cold and grey Christmas Day. When they reached the alleyway there were police cars parked at angles across the front of it and scene-of-crime tape hanging from lamp-post to lamp-post.

Rose stood with her arms crossed. Joshua had his hands in his pockets, pulling the front of his coat tightly together so that the bunched up fabric covered the stain. Rose's fingers were icy. She looked up and down the street. Houses and shops, parked cars and wheelie bins, completely ordinary.

But Skeggsie had been attacked and left to die in an alley off this street.

She let her eyes drop to the ground. She stared at the

grey paving stones and felt the tears gather again. She pulled a wad of toilet paper from her pocket and pushed it against her eyelids, a sob wrenching out of her.

The police were going in and out, looking business-like. A car pulled up, double parking by one of the squad cars. The driver got out and Skeggsie's father emerged from the passenger side. Joshua stiffened and took a step forward. There was nowhere to go, though – they were flat against the scene-of-crime tape. The two men walked into the alley.

They waited.

Other people came and there was a burst of conversation as they heard about what had happened. 'Some kid got stabbed last night! Was it drugs? It was probably drug-related. Or to do with a girl. Yeah, maybe it was a girl.' Rose glanced up at Joshua. He was staring straight ahead, his face rigid, as if he couldn't hear a word.

Skeggsie's father came out of the alley. He saw them and walked across. Joshua crossed his arms, hiding the bloodstain.

'Joshua, lad, I don't know what to say . . . Or to think . . . I . . .'

'We found him,' Joshua said, his voice shaking. 'We did everything we could.'

'I know you did. The officers told me. I can't believe what's happened. My Darren, my boy,' he stopped. 'He wasn't the type to get in a fight . . .'

'He wasn't. He would never have started anything.'

'You were a good friend, Joshua. Don't think I don't know what you did . . .'

'No, he was a good friend to me when I needed it. The best.'

Bob Skeggs looked around. His eyes were glittering. Rose looked away. He made a coughing sound and stepped back from them.

'I have to go now. There are procedures to be followed and I may be out of touch today but I'll contact you.'

Rose looked down and thought of her words to Skeggsie the night before. *If I'm honest, I don't always like you very much.*

'Did they tell you anything? How it happened?' Joshua said.

'Not really. Too soon, lad. Too soon to draw conclusions.'

'I'll ring you tomorrow,' Joshua said.

Bob walked off towards the car that had brought him there. Within minutes they had driven off. Rose saw the young officer then, the one who'd come first the previous evening. He walked towards them.

'So sorry about your friend,' he said.

Rose gave a shaky smile.

'Is there any information about him? Have the police found out what happened?'

'It's ongoing. We've set up an incident room . . .'

Rose had stopped listening because Joshua's expression had changed. She looked around, following his gaze. A group of young men were coming towards them. Rose could see Martin and some others. At the back was Rory Spenser.

'I'll tell you one thing, though,' the policeman said, lowering his voice. 'We found the murder weapon.'

Joshua looked back at the policeman.

'Knife?'

'Yep. It's with forensics.'

Joshua looked ashen. He stared into space and then seemed startled to see the others coming towards them. Martin was the first to reach them.

'Josh, mate. I can't believe it.'

The others followed. Rose saw that Rory hung back, a few metres away and began to fiddle with the scene-of-crime tape. Joshua seemed not to know who Martin was and Martin frowned at Rose.

'We only heard this morning. We were out of it last night and an hour ago I got a text from my mate, Roger, who heard about it from his old man who's a porter in the hospital.'

Rose nodded, her mouth too dry to speak. Martin put his hand out to Joshua but then drew it back. Joshua just stared at Rory Spenser who had his back to them. A ring-tone sounded. It was a pop song, loud and raucous and it made everyone, even the policeman, turn round. It was

Rory's phone. He took it out and answered the call, his voice as casual as if he were standing in a queue for the supermarket till, not in front of a crime scene.

'Oh hi!' he said. 'What you up to?'

Joshua tensed, his jaw rigid.

'Josh,' Martin said, stepping towards him.

But Joshua had sprung, his big coat flying out. He ran towards Rory Spenser and jumped on his back, pushing him forward face down on the ground. There was a grunting sound and then Rory's phone shot out of his hand and skidded along the road. Rose was shocked. Joshua was punching the side of Rory's head.

'Oi!' the policeman shouted.

Martin and one of the others went across and took hold of Joshua's arms and dragged him off Rory. Rory scrabbled to his feet and backed away, holding his jaw, scooping up his phone as he went.

Joshua shook free and stood unsteadily. The policeman walked across to Rory and spoke quietly. Rory shrugged his shoulders and walked off. The policeman came back to Joshua.

'I don't want to arrest you, mate. I can see you're all over the place. Get off home now. Calm down.'

Joshua looked at Martin.

'He was stabbed, Marty.'

'Mate, I'm sorry, I don't know what to say.'

'I know Spenser had something to do with this.'

Martin began to shake his head.

'You tell him to watch his back because when I'm absolutely sure I'll come for him. This time he'll pay properly for what he's done.'

Martin didn't answer. He looked down at Joshua's coat. Joshua's eyes dropped and focused on the stain as if he was seeing it for the first time. It seemed to appal him and he pulled at the buttons and shook the coat off. Then he bundled it up and threw it on the ground and walked away.

'He's lost it,' Martin said quietly. 'There's no way Rory would do this. No way.'

Martin beckoned his friends and they went in the direction that Rory had gone moments earlier. Rose looked at Joshua's coat on the ground. She bent down and picked it up then she followed him home.

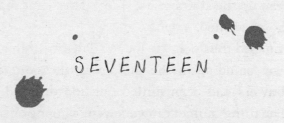

SEVENTEEN

Rose placed Joshua's coat on a chair in the kitchen.

Distressed, she looked around. The table was covered in stuff that had not been put away over the previous couple of days – cups, glasses, plates and papers. By the door was Poppy's bowl with half-eaten food in it. Her water bowl was almost empty and there was something floating there. It made Rose's stomach turn slightly. The sink had dirty dishes in it and the milk had been left out on the side.

She walked into the living room. Her duvet was on the sofa and there were clothes of hers that she'd left over the armchair. There were glasses on the mantelpiece from two nights before. The room smelled fusty and she saw the remains of toast on a plate on top of the TV.

How had it got like this?

From upstairs she heard the sound of Joshua moving around. She stood still and listened. The door slammed as he went into his uncle's bedroom. Then she heard the sound of things being dropped one after the other. She flinched as they thudded on to the floor above her.

She ran up the stairs.

'Josh?' she called.

She opened the door.

He was standing in the middle of the room. All the desk drawers had been pulled out and dropped on the floor. The filing cabinet drawers were hanging open and it looked as though their files had been scooped out and chucked.

'Go away, Rose,' Joshua said, without looking at her. 'I need to be on my own.'

'What are you doing?'

'Go away.'

'I can't.'

'GO AWAY, ROSE,' he shouted at her.

She stood her ground. He glared at her for a few seconds then he seemed to shrink back. His voice had an unnatural calm when he spoke.

'I'm getting rid of it all. All this stuff, all this crap that I've had my head into for the last few days. Ever since I heard that Stu called out Dad's name I've been obsessed with it.'

'That's understandable . . .'

'I've thought of nothing else.'

'I know . . .'

'And you know why?'

'You were trying to work out what happened to Stu on the cliff.'

'No. I was trying to work my way back to the note-books. This accident, him falling over the side of the cliff, that wasn't enough for me to deal with. I thought I was trying to work out what happened but the moment I heard Dad's name, the second there was a reason to go back to Dad and Kathy's disappearance I focused on that. I turned the house upside down. I couldn't think of anything else.'

'You thought it might give a clue to what happened to Stuart.'

'No, Rose. I didn't. The minute I thought I could stop thinking about what happened on the cliff I dropped it. Just like when I went to London in September I never came back for a weekend. Not once. Stu must have thought . . .'

Joshua leant on the extended drawer of the filing cabinet.

'Josh, this has been so hard for you . . .'

'I just dropped him. He cared for me . . . At least I thought he did. I thought I knew him but . . .'

Rose stepped forward. She put her hand on his shoulder and it felt hot. He shook it off.

'Nothing you can say can change the way I've been. Stu was my dad for five years but that wasn't enough for me. I wanted my real dad. Remember him? The guy who faked his own disappearance, the one who left me on my own.'

'Josh.'

He was shaking, his jaw trembling. Rose took a step up to him and pulled him away from the filing cabinet. She put her arms around him. She hugged him tightly but he was rigid, the muscles in his back tense. It felt as if he was paralysed.

'Josh, Josh,' she whispered, soothing.

'But that's not the worst,' he said, shaking her off, stepping across the debris on the floor, walking out of the room. 'I dragged Skeggs into it.'

She followed him. He went into his room and sat on the bed, his legs apart, his elbows on his knees, looking down at the floor, like he'd done in the hospital the previous night. She leant against his door. She'd seen him upset before but now there was a kind of hysteria in his words. After a few seconds he spoke again, his throat thick with emotion.

'I pulled Skeggsie into it. He wasn't unwilling but I made it a big part of his life. I leant on him completely and never once did I step back and ask myself whether he wouldn't be better moving on. He's had this new mate at college, Eddie? You've heard him talk about him?'

Rose nodded.

'There've been times when I knew he was going to some gig or meeting Eddie and I said, *Oh, not tonight, Skeggs, mate, I thought we could work on the notebooks.* I pulled him back. I liked the fact that he was my sounding board, my *confidant*.'

'He liked it too.'

'I know. We had a sort of unspoken bargain. We were like brothers only not related but we were bound together by stuff. He was my . . .'

Joshua trembled and Rose stepped forward but he held his hand up in front of him to keep her back.

'I took my eye off the ball,' he said through tears. 'We came up here and I knew there was history here for Skeggs but I was so wound up in all this, I was so busy with all this . . .'

'He *insisted* on being involved.'

'Ever since we got up here it's been Stu this, Stu that and then back to the notebooks, back to the old obsession. Never mind that someone had decided to settle old scores with Skeggs. I couldn't see it. I was too busy.'

'It's not your fault.'

'It is my fault, Rose. You don't get it. I look out for Skeggs.' He stood up and began to pace up and down. 'Not down in London – there, he's OK – but when he's up here no one touches him. Everyone knows. Anything happens to him they deal with me, that's how it's been for years.'

Rose thought of the previous night in the pub smoking area. Skeggsie had told Joshua then *You have to let me fight my own battles, mate.*

'I'll find out who's done this,' he said, walking up to the wall and slamming the side of his fist into it. 'I won't rest till I find out.'

She walked up behind him. She put her hands on his elbows. She guided him back to the bed.

'You're exhausted. You can't think straight about this until you've rested.'

He let himself be manhandled and sat down on the bed. Then he seemed to weaken and lean against her.

'Lie down.'

He did what she said. She took his boots off then pulled the duvet over.

'Try and sleep, just for a few hours.'

He grabbed her hand.

'Don't leave me, Rosie . . .'

She frowned and looked down at him. He looked so lost, so battered. She took off her own boots and her jumper and got in beside him. She turned on her side so that he was against her back. He hugged her and she felt him kissing her hair. She pulled the duvet up and they both lay there, clamped together.

Somewhere in the distance she thought she could hear church bells and she remembered, before she went to sleep, that it was Christmas Day.

When she woke up it was dark. She was hot, the duvet up to her nose. She realised then that she was on her own. Joshua had got up. She turned over and the whole awful thing came back to her. Skeggsie was dead. She pulled her knees up and hugged herself. A few days ago she had been convinced that things were as bad as they could get. How could she have known then that they had darker places to go?

She thought back to the previous night. It had been a mess, everyone feeling out of sorts. Skeggsie had been on edge, especially when Rory Spenser came into the pub. Joshua arrived, wound up by the discovery of his uncle's letter to the solicitor. Then there had been the horrible scene in the pub smoking area. Joshua enraged at Rory Spenser, the row with Skeggsie who had said *Sometimes it's like you two are the only people in the world who've ever felt loss*. Skeggsie had thrown his lot in with Joshua. He'd been happy to put aside his own life to pursue their search. But in doing that his life had been disregarded.

After all the arguing and fighting and hurt feelings he'd gone out of the pub to get Joshua and bring him back. He'd slipped out of the noise and the lights and beery atmosphere into the cold night. He'd headed for Joshua's house, no doubt sidestepping partygoers. He'd turned off the Promenade and somehow he'd been drawn into the alleyway between the shops.

Rose closed her eyes tightly.

She and Joshua knew loss but this was different. Skeggsie had been so close, so near. She'd seen him moments before it had happened. It almost seemed as though she could have put her hand out and stopped him. Maybe she could have said, *I'll come too. We'll walk together.* Or she could have persuaded Skeggsie to give Joshua time. *Come and play some darts*, she could have said, *Josh'll come round*. And he did come round. Joshua's anger had fallen away and he'd come back to the pub.

The door opened and light poked into the room.

'Rose,' Joshua whispered, 'I phoned the hospital and left a message for my uncle. I just said there'd been an accident.'

'That's good.'

'Now I'm taking Poppy for a walk.'

'Wait for me,' she said. 'I want to come.'

She staggered up, out of the warm bed, picked up her jumper and boots and stumbled towards the bathroom. She rinsed her face for the second time that day. She combed her fingers through her hair and went downstairs. Joshua was waiting by the front door. He was wearing the leather bomber jacket that he'd bought for his uncle as a Christmas present. It gave her a start to look at it. It made her think of his other coat gory with blood.

'What time is it?' she said.

'Five o'clock.'

It seemed later. She put her coat on and Joshua held a scarf out for her to wrap round her neck. Then he opened the front door. A veil of snow wafted in and she did her coat up and stepped outside into it. The cold air woke her up and she walked quickly to keep pace with Joshua. He pulled Poppy across and held her lead with one hand.

With the other he grasped hers and pulled it into the pocket of the bomber jacket. She held his hand tightly.

They walked on, coming up to the alleyway, deserted now, just the scene-of-crime tape flapping in the wind. He let go of her hand and walked towards the opening between the shops. She followed him. Poppy was straining on the lead to go further. Neither of them spoke for a few moments.

'I've decided,' Joshua said eventually. 'From now on I'm going to spend every minute trying to find out what happened to Skeggs.'

She nodded.

'My uncle, the notebooks, all that will be put on hold. I won't think about any of it until I find out who's responsible.'

'I'll help you.'

'I knew you would, Rosie,' he said, his hand squeezing hers.

'We'll do it together,' she said.

He stared at her, his eyes dark. He lifted one of his hands up to her face and touched her skin.

'I'm not going to rest until I find out who did it.'

'I know,' she said, taking his hand and kissing it.

He pulled her to him and hugged her, his arm like a vice around her back.

'I owe him this,' he said, stifling a sob.

'We both do,' Rose said.

EIGHTEEN

On Boxing Day Rose and Joshua were called to the station to give statements to the police. They were there for most of the morning. They returned to the house and took Poppy for a walk. In the afternoon Joshua slept on the sofa, his feet hanging off the end. Rose put the single duvet from her bed over him and then went into the kitchen and called Anna to tell her what had happened. Her grandmother was shocked and asked if Rose wanted her to come up to Newcastle. Rose gently declined the offer. Her grandmother sounded bewildered at the news and after ending the call Rose wondered what she must have thought about her grand-daughter. After coming home from boarding school six months before there seemed to have been a string of violent deaths associated with her. Anna was unsettled by these events; her safe world, her music, her friends, her charity work, her house in Belsize Park, was not so solid now. Rose seemed to *attract* death. It left her feeling responsible in some way, as if her very presence made something bad happen.

Now there were deaths that came from the past. The Butterfly Murder. Judy Greaves, a ten-year-old girl, murdered and left in a room full of mounted butterflies. These things hung in Rose's thoughts like heavy black clouds.

In the afternoon Joshua went to the hospital. He asked her if she minded if he went alone. They'd missed their visit on Christmas Day. Joshua wanted to talk through what had happened to Skeggsie with his uncle. When the front door shut after him she was mildly relieved. The thought of seeing Stuart Johnson after everything that had happened was making her a little nervous. His confession about the murder of Simon Lister was on her mind and she wondered if she would ever be able to act normally towards him; as if he was just some nice uncle of Joshua's that she had never met, not this man she'd been thinking about and talking about for days.

When Joshua got back he told her how his uncle was and how shocked he'd been about the news of Skeggsie's death. She asked a few other questions but Joshua seemed tired and dispirited. The energy with which he had started the day had disappeared. Later in the evening he put the bottle of whisky by his side and poured it into his glass from time to time. Rose watched him with apprehension.

'Tomorrow we make a start,' Joshua said, his words slurred.

He went to bed before her. She let Poppy out into the garden and then went up to bed herself. She hesitated as she passed his door. On Christmas Day they'd slept together for hours but the previous night they'd each gone to their own rooms. It was as if it hadn't happened. She reached out to the handle of his door.

Why not go in?

Why not get in beside him? Hold him close?

She walked on, though, into the box room and her single bed.

She slept soundly and felt fuzzy-headed and dry-mouthed when she woke up the next morning. Joshua, it appeared, had been up for ages. The half bottle of whisky had had little effect on him. He'd showered and changed his clothes and told her that he was getting going. He was busy and looked organised and she felt a little distanced from him as though the closeness of the previous two days was not needed now that they were *getting going.*

'We'll clear the house up. I have to sort out my uncle's room for when he comes home?'

'Did the hospital say when?'

'A couple of days.

'And Rosie, I've decided, when Stu comes home I'm not going to mention the Butterfly Murder. I'm going to put all the stuff away and it'll be as if we never found it.'

'Can you do that?'

'For the time being. We need to completely focus on Skeggsie. And even after that I still have to get my head around what it all means in relation to Dad and Kathy. But I can't do that now. *We* can't do it now. So I don't want to let Stu know that I know anything.'

She shrugged in agreement.

'Bob Skeggs is coming round later so we can find out what's happening in the investigation.'

Joshua worked upstairs and Rose took the downstairs rooms. She started with the kitchen and filled up a number of rubbish bags. She paused and then decided to clean out the cupboards. She took the mugs and plates out, scrubbed the interior, and replaced them in some sort of order. The living room didn't take long. She got the vacuum cleaner out and moved the furniture and tidied.

Then she went into the garden. There was dog mess to clear up.

Poppy leapt around her, thinking it was a game.

Back inside she paused. She considered taking a rest but immediately felt the weight of everything pushing at her temples. If she stopped she would just start thinking again. She found other things to do. The cupboard under the stairs was a mess. She took the coats out and tidied them on to hangers. She struggled with the vacuum cleaner and pointed the nozzle into the corners of the cupboard and came across a pair of walking boots that were encrusted with mud. She took them to the sink and started to clean off the dirt. It was a mindless job, getting a knife into the treads of the sole and shifting the mud. She wished she had a whole row of boots to clean.

It was robotic work and it filled the time and every half hour that passed took them further away from the events of Christmas Eve. About two she made some toast and took it upstairs to Joshua. He was in his room looking at his laptop. He took the toast and nibbled at the corners. She stood awkwardly, finding it impossible to settle on any conversation. Joshua was looking at her but she knew he was not *seeing* her. His sight was somewhere else, maybe still in that dark alley.

Soon after Bob Skeggs arrived.

Rose held Poppy back as he came in. He looked white-faced and only had on a suit jacket over trousers even though it was bitterly cold. He kept saying, 'Thank you for what you did for Darren.' Rose felt full of emotion and was afraid that if she said a single word it would all pour out so she just nodded and patted him on the shoulder. Joshua came down the stairs two at a time. He took him into the living room and when the door closed behind them the hallway seemed warmer, as if he had taken the cold with him.

Rose stood for a moment and heard the murmuring of voices. She was grateful for the sound of conversation. It was so much better than the stark silence of the morning.

She went upstairs. Joshua had been scrupulous in clearing up. She looked in on Stuart's study and saw that all the drawers were back in place. She sat down at the desk and opened each one and saw piles of files with felt-tip writing on them. Everything, it seemed, had been sorted into newly labelled files. Joshua had tidied up Stuart's life – *Bills, Salary, Union, Classic Cars, Bank Statements, Debts*.

When Bob Skeggs left the house Rose went downstairs. She found Joshua sitting in the living room. On the coffee table were a set of car keys and Skeggsie's laptop.

'How's his dad?' she said.

He shrugged.

'Bob wants me to use the Mini. And look after the flat. For the time being.'

Joshua reached over and picked up Skeggsie's keys. He clutched them tightly as though someone might want to take them from him. She saw the veins on the back of his hands stand out, the muscles in his forearm tense. He stood up, putting the keys in his pocket.

'How come he's brought the laptop?'

'He wants me to contact Skeggsie's tutors and friends. Fill them in on what happened. I can't really face doing it now. How many of them are going to want to have an email about this over Christmas?'

'And the case? Have the police made any progress?'

What she meant was, *Have they found the killer?*

'They've done a lot of door-to-door stuff and they've interviewed people in the pub, particularly those who were in the smoking area. Rory Spenser and Martin have been asked to go in for a formal interview this afternoon.'

'They've done a lot.'

'The son of an ex-Detective Inspector. They'll do anything to find the killer when it is one of their own.'

These words chimed with Rose. Skeggsie had said the very same thing to her a couple of months before when she first knew him. The status of a murder victim was important. The son of a policeman was high; a boy or girl from a single parent family on a council estate was not so important. No one would ever admit to this but it was true.

'There's nothing we can do until all these statements are in. We should go out and get some food. There's nothing left in the kitchen.'

Joshua drove the Mini. He headed for a shopping centre and parked. When he got out he seemed lost, not sure where to go.

'There's a Co-op,' Rose said. 'We can get some food there.'

He took a step but then stopped.

'I don't think I can . . .'

He looked a bit nauseous.

'I might see someone that I know and I'm not up to talking to anyone.'

'You stay in the car. I'll get the stuff.'

She left him there and walked into the brightly lit mall. Once inside she bought the groceries she thought they needed. When she got to the till she saw that she hadn't bought any fruit or vegetables just cheese and bread, bacon and chicken, pizza and eggs. She frowned. It was too late to go back. Food was the last thing on their minds anyway. On her way out she passed the newspaper stand. She was startled by the headlines: **Police Inspector's Son Slain; Christmas Stabbing; Youth Crime – Another Stabbing; Son of Policeman Killed.**

The murder had made the national press. It surprised her. Other killings that she'd been involved in had barely made the local paper. She suddenly thought of Eddie, in London. Skeggsie's new friend. Did he already know about Skeggsie's death?

She walked back into the mall and paused momentarily to transfer her bags from one hand to the other. Her attention was taken by a couple who had come out of Mothercare. The woman was linking the man's arm and he was holding a couple of Mothercare bags. He was talking and smiling and the woman was nodding, her ponytail going up and down. She watched them walk off. They were familiar but she couldn't place them.

Then in a flash she knew who they were. It was Greg Tyler and his wife, Susie. Stuart's old girlfriend and her husband. She walked after them towards the car park. They were in front of her. Greg had his arm around his wife's shoulders. From the back they looked like a couple of young lovers. It wasn't how Susie had described her relationship with her husband when she came to see Joshua on Friday night.

She peeled away from them towards the area where the Mini was parked.

'Martin's just sent me a text,' Joshua said when she reached the car. 'He wants me to go and see him. He says he's got some information.'

Rose put the food in the back and then got into the car.

'You all right?' he said.

She nodded. As they drove off she saw Susie and Greg Tyler walking out of the car park and away from the shopping mall. There was a bounce in Greg's step, the Mothercare bags swinging from his hand. Rose thought back to the night when Susie came round to see Joshua. Hadn't she said then that she and Greg couldn't have any children of their own? Hadn't that been one of the reasons that they had drifted apart?

Rose shrugged. Maybe Susie was buying a gift for a friend.

'What you thinking about?' Joshua said. 'Skeggsie?'

Rose nodded. It was easier than trying to explain.

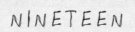

NINETEEN

Ten minutes later they were at Martin's door.

'How you doing?' he said to Joshua.

Joshua grunted.

They followed him into a warm kitchen.

'Mum and Dad are out. You want a hot drink?'

Joshua shook his head. So did Rose.

'Sit down at least.'

Joshua pulled out a chair and sat on the edge of it, his knees sticking out at an awkward angle so that Rose had to step across his feet in order to sit down. Martin stayed standing with his back to the fridge. Rose noticed there were word magnets stuck to the door. Hundreds of words, some in lines, some in random groups. She had to pull her eyes away to stop herself reading them.

'I've just got back from giving my statement to the police. Me and Rory went together and I wanted to tell you what he told me. I know you think he did Skeggs but he didn't. He left after the ruck out the back of the pub which you had a hand in, Josh. He went off on his own and he said he hooked up with Michelle Hinds. They went to the Beer Hut, that pub at the jetty? Used to be the Fisherman's Rest? His brother was there with some of his mates. They stayed there till gone midnight then he went round to George Knightly's. That was the party most people ended up at. We all saw him arrive about twelve thirty. He was with Michelle in the pub and then the two of them came to George's. He wasn't on his own. He couldn't have done anything.'

'Michelle Hinds?' Joshua said.

'Yeah. They are an on-off sort of thing.'

'She's *with* him?'

'Not really. They're mates and sometimes . . .'

'With *Rory*?'

'You know what Michelle's like,' Martin said, his eyes flicking towards Rose and back to Joshua. 'You kept her company once or twice as I remember. He said he met her as he came out of the Lighthouse and she took his arm and they walked towards the Beer Hut.'

'So we've only got Michelle Hinds' word for it.'

'Why would she lie?'

Joshua sighed.

'In any case the police will check other people at the pub. And there's his brother.'

'He'd lie for him!'

'Go and ask Michelle. She still lives with her sister in Petty's Lane.'

184

Joshua stood up. Martin carried on talking.

'Rory's changed. Don't get me wrong – he's still a total loser but it's all mouth. He just says it to keep up a front.'

'But why couldn't he just leave Skeggs alone?'

'Because no one else round here takes him seriously. Skeggs comes back and Rory's got someone to wind up. But he wouldn't stab him. He just wouldn't.'

'When did his brother get out of prison?'

'A few months back. Look, I told you, Rory's been going to my old boxing club. He's trying to make something of himself. He's got a mouth on him but that's all.'

'Where is Rory now?'

'He's back at his mum's. You shouldn't go and see him, Josh. Not the way you're feeling now. Go and see Michelle. Talk to her.'

Rose looked at the two of them. They were standing a few steps apart. On Friday night, in the pub, they'd hugged each other, pleased to be meeting up again. Now there was a barrier between them.

'You all right, Rose?' Martin said.

She nodded and gave him a weak smile. He'd done nothing wrong, just become embroiled in other people's fights.

Martin stood at his front door as they drove off. Rose raised her hand in a tiny wave.

'How do you know Michelle?'

'From the girls' school. She had a boyfriend at our

school, then another, then another. She was never short of company.'

'Even with you?'

'I spent some time with her. Lots of boys did.'

Rose felt a pang of sadness. She didn't like to think of Joshua like just any other boy. She didn't picture him as a sweaty teen in the back of a car trying to get his hand up a girl's blouse. Not that she had ever had such an experience but she had heard girls from her boarding school talking about it. Her silence was heavy with things she wanted to say, to ask, but now wasn't the right time.

They pulled up outside a row of small cottages. There were Christmas lights hanging from the guttering that shimmered in the darkness. The front door opened and Michelle stood there. She looked as though she was all ready to go out somewhere, her hair and make-up the same as Rose had seen them in the pub the previous Friday night. She had a fitted top on over some jeans and high heels.

'Martin sent me a text and said you were coming,' she said, loudly, confidently. 'I could do with a break as it goes. How about a ride?'

'Get in,' Josh said.

Michelle ducked back inside and came out with a coat and bag. Rose held the passenger seat up so that she could get into the back. When Rose sat down and the car moved off she could smell heavy perfume.

'Don't suppose I can smoke?' Michelle said.

'No.'

'Can't smoke here, can't smoke there, can't smoke anywhere.'

'Where do you want to go?'

'Let's go to Cullercoats. The old cafe. Nobody minds me smoking there.'

They drove in silence and within minutes pulled up into a parking spot not far from where she and Joshua had walked Poppy on the day before Christmas Eve. They got out of the car, Michelle emerging unruffled from the back seat and marching ahead, her cigarette in her hand. They headed for the boarded up cafe. The outside area was partly sheltered by an awning with brick walls on each side and looked out on to the North Sea. There were benches and tables, all fixed to the ground, some of them in the open air but most covered. The area had the look of frequent use, with crushed-up beer cans thrown into the corner, cigarette butts everywhere.

'Heard about your uncle. That was awful. Now this. Your friend. A bad time for you, Josh.'

'Yeah.'

There was quiet and Rose felt awkward. She waited for Joshua to speak but he said nothing. He looked mildly embarrassed.

'I'm Rose, by the way,' she said.

'I saw you in the pub the other night. You're not from round here.'

'I live in London,' Rose said and looked around at the desolate cafe. 'Is it closed for the winter?'

'It's been closed for a couple of years,' Michelle said, sitting on a bench, lighting up. 'Someone said that it had a new owner so I suppose we'll have to find somewhere else soon.'

'Can't you go to a pub or something?' Joshua said. 'You're not fourteen any more.'

'As I recall you used to like coming up here. Especially when it was just you and me, Josh.'

Joshua made a face. Rose looked away. Michelle was sucking on her cigarette.

'Christmas Eve. You were with Rory at the Fisherman's Rest,' Joshua said.

'Called the Beer Hut now. Nice and trendy.'

'What time were you with him?'

Michelle exhaled, blowing the smoke to the side.

'I'm sorry about your friend. I never knew him. Darren, was that his name?'

Joshua nodded.

'In London, wasn't he? At university?'

She pronounced it in syllables, u-ni-ver-sit-y. As if it was another world.

'What time did you meet him?'

'Don't be in such a rush, Josh. You got no time to talk with me? No time for a little bit of chit-chat.'

'My best mate is dead. I don't feel like chit-chat.'

''Course you don't. I understand that. But it's not just now, is it? You were a nice boy, polite, sweet, as long as you got something in return. Soon as you got that you had no time for chit-chat with Michelle. Walk past me in the street. No time to even say hello. Why was that? Exactly?'

'I don't know what you mean. This isn't the time to talk about *that* . . .'

'There never will be any time to talk about it. What do my feelings matter? A girl's bit of hurt pride don't measure up, I know. But it's there all the same.'

'And is Rory Spenser different?' Joshua said angrily.

'Rory's a mate. Sometimes it's a bit more than that. I saw him outside the Lighthouse on Christmas Eve and he was upset, angry so I says, *Come down the Fisherman's with me*, so he did. We saw his brother Sean in there. He bought us a drink and then he cleared off. After twelve we started to walk to Georgie Knightley's. I dunno what time we got there. About half hour later. That's all I got to say.'

Michelle stood up. She threw the butt of her cigarette away.

'The trouble with you, Josh-u-a, is that you think you're something special. You go to the grammar school, you get your exams, you get into u-ni-ver-sit-y and you think you're better than everyone else. You might know more, you might speak with a nice accent but I remember when you and me were sitting up here on summer evenings looking out at the sea. Then you wasn't better than me. Then you was sweet and kind. You might think that what we did up here was just nothing to me but you were wrong. You might believe all the other boys in your school who said they did it too but I only spent time up here with kids I really liked and all I hoped was that when they saw me or passed me in the street they might say hello and stop for a bit of chit-chat. I'll be on my way now. Don't worry about giving me a lift back. I'll walk.'

She walked off, away from the cafe. Joshua seemed stunned. Rose looked at him with annoyance. She ran after Michelle.

'Wait,' she called. 'Hang on. Michelle!'

Michelle turned round. Her hair was blowing back in the wind.

'Joshua is really upset now. That's why he's being . . . He's so wound up with what happened to Skeggsie he can't think straight.'

'But you don't get it, Rose. He's always been like this with me. Ever since . . .' Michelle gestured towards the cafe.

'He was a schoolboy then. Now he's different.'

'How come he hardly had a word to say to me in the pub on Friday night? Why did he blank me then?'

'I don't know. Maybe it's because he's totally embarrassed at how he acted. That's the only thing I can think of. The Josh I know is so the complete opposite of what you're describing. I can only think that it's embarrassment.'

Joshua had come up to them.

'I'm sorry, Michelle.'

Michelle gave a smile.

'Really?' she said.

'I've been a total prat.'

'So next time you see me in the pub you'll say hello?'

'I'll buy you a beer and we'll talk.'

She stared at him. It was hard to know whether she'd stopped being angry.

'OK. That's a deal.'

'Do you want a lift?'

'No. I'm heading for the Royal Hotel. I'm on duty at six. Trainee Receptionist!'

They began to walk towards the car. Michelle continued to talk.

'Now me and Rory was together from about eleven until about two when we left Georgie's party. I will say one thing, though. He was upset. He was furious at you, Josh, not so much the other boy, Darren. He was ranting about you to Sean. Then Sean got angry. He left soon after.'

'Sean?'

'Rory ain't violent any more. I don't think he would stab your friend. But *Sean* might.'

They were at the car.

'You sure you don't want a lift home?'

'No, I'm doing extra evenings at the Royal this week.

Christmas period a lot of staff are off. It's extra cash for me so I don't mind. See you. And you, Rose. Thanks for the chat. Oh, and you won't find Sean Spenser at home. Rory told me he hasn't seen him since Christmas Eve. That's what happens with Sean. Sometimes they don't see him for weeks.'

'Thanks.'

Michelle walked off and gave a backwards wave. Rose couldn't help but smile at the brash, forthright girl. She looked towards Joshua but saw that he had already got back into the car and was starting up the ignition.

She got in and they drove off.

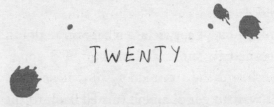

TWENTY

Joshua made a call to Bob Skeggs as soon as they got back to the house. His voice was rapid and forceful. Rose could hear bits of the conversation and felt wearied by it all. 'He left the Lighthouse at eleven . . . Rory Spenser with Michelle Hinds . . . Sean Spenser hasn't been seen since . . . The Fisherman's Rest now called the Beer Hut . . . Skeggsie's body found at eleven forty-five . . . Party at George Knightley's . . .'

She headed into the kitchen and put the shopping away. On the table was Skeggsie's laptop. She booted it up and entered Skeggsie's password. Then she went upstairs to get her own laptop and brought it back down and placed it alongside Skeggsie's. Both machines came to life, one lagging after the other. After a few moments she felt Joshua standing behind her. He seemed charged, pent up, as if he needed to be *doing* something. She didn't know what to say to him. He spoke first.

'Bob's got some autopsy details and early forensics. I'd

said I'd go round to his place and have a look at them. You can come if you want.'

'No, I'll stay here and get on with sending these messages.'

'Thanks, Rose. I appreciate what you're doing.'

She turned to smile at him but he'd gone. Seconds later she heard the front door shut. It seemed as if he couldn't wait to get out. She turned back to the computer. The first thing she wanted to do was to write to Eddie. She was sending the message from *her* laptop. She did not want Eddie, or any of the college tutors, to receive an email from Skeggsie's laptop. She made a number of starts.

Dear Eddie, you don't know me but I'm a friend of Skeggsie . . .

Dear Eddie, I'm writing as a very close friend of Darren Skeggs . . .

Eddie, my name is Rose Smith and I knew Skeggsie well and I was with him on the night that he died . . .

When she'd finally composed it she pressed *Send* then sat back.

She gradually felt herself loosen up, her shoulders softening, her breathing slowing down. Being with Joshua all day had made her tense and tight. It had been full on. Sorting out the house, seeing Bob Skeggs, going to the shopping mall, going to Martin's and then seeing Michelle. It had been a day of sharp edges, Joshua blustering into them, Rose trying to ease round the difficult parts, wanting to make things easier not harder.

But it was always going to be harder for Joshua because Skeggsie had been his friend. She'd only known Skeggsie through Joshua. She didn't have the deep feelings that he had. She was upset, of course. The brutal way he had died had shocked and angered her but in the end she would get over it whereas it would stay with Joshua for ever.

She made herself a drink. She stood very still while the kettle boiled and listened to the silence of the house. Poppy was lying by the back door, her nose pointing towards the garden. The dog had a way of letting people know what she wanted to do. She was reminded then of the dog that she had seen in the silver SUV. When she'd been sitting in the beach shelter she'd seen the woman with the dog as she walked from the doors of the Royal Hotel towards her car.

The silver SUV that was owned by Beaufort Holdings.

It was something they'd put on the back burner while Skeggsie's death was being investigated.

Poppy was making impatient noises so Rose stepped across and unlocked the door to let her out. It was less cold now, the snow and ice had slipped away without her noticing. The kettle was steaming and then turned itself off. The click sounded loud in the silent kitchen. She poured the water into a cup and added a drop of milk. Then she stood very still and luxuriated in the quiet of the room. The eye of the storm. Joshua had taken all the stress and upset with him. He would be back soon and then it would all start again.

After she drank her tea she settled down and looked at Skeggsie's email history over the last few weeks. She then sent messages to each of the people that he had had regular contact with, telling them what had happened. Most people, she thought, would already know as it had been in the national newspapers but still she gave some details and said some things about how important Skeggsie's course had been to him. She also said how much his family and friends would miss him. At this she stopped and felt her emotions rising. She sat very still for a few seconds holding the feelings down then she finished the emails.

She sat back.

She didn't expect any replies and yet there, in her inbox, was a message from Eddie.

Dear Rose, thank you so much for this. I knew of course, I'd seen it in the papers. I couldn't believe it. I didn't know Skeggsie very long but I thought of him as a mate and I liked his style and he was a brilliant animator. What a useless waste. Eddie.

Rose closed her laptop down. She'd sent as many messages as she felt like sending. Then she looked at Skeggsie's screen. Among his email files there was one for Eddie. She clicked on it. There was a long list. She had

no intention of looking at any of Skeggsie's private corre-
spondence. She was only interested in the last couple of
messages. The subject line pinpointed the ones she was
interested in. They both held the registration of the SUV,
GT50 DNT.

She clicked on the earliest one, sent on Sunday, after
she'd told Skeggsie about the car.

Hi Skeggs, how's it going up there in the cold north?
Can you understand the accent :-(

Rose smiled. The email went on in that jokey style
then at the end there was some reference to the registration number.

I've got your keys so I'll go round to the flat tomorrow
and have a look at the programme you mentioned
(another one of your breaking and entering gizmos – you
should sell it on the black market, you'd make a fortune).
Once I've input the data I'll leave it to search. I'll take
your word for it that it's not traceable (at least not to
me!). I trust you. I'll leave it a day and go back and look.
I'll let you know if I find anything. Ed :-)

Eddie had keys to Skeggsie's flat. That surprised Rose.
Skeggsie had been so paranoid about the flat. When she
first knew him he insisted on the doors being locked and
unlocked every time someone came in and went out.

Recently he'd become less suspicious.

She sat very still, thinking of the irony of this. He'd
made a friend apart from Joshua. He'd given out the

keys to his flat, trusted Eddie to go in there when he wasn't at home. He'd become keen to take on his own battles, telling Joshua to keep out of things. Then someone had ripped all that new-found confidence away from him.

She looked at the next email from Eddie on the following day.

Skeggs, checked the computer. Got info on your mystery SUV. It's registered to a company called Beaufort Holdings Ltd, link here. Looks above board but you better be the judge. The programme disengaged itself after searching so there shouldn't be any comeback. I'm with my sister for Christmas lunch but I'll have my phone so if you want anything else just call. Ed :-)

Rose clicked on the link. There were photographs of country houses fronted by iron gates with CCTV cameras.

Beaufort Holdings is a well regarded security company which offers on-site property protection and manned security services. Working mainly in the east of England we have experience of all electronic security solutions. We serve a range of discerning customers. We provide the highest quality tried and tested security systems for gated communities and bespoke systems for individual homeowners. Our business embraces a strong focus on service and partnership.

She scanned the pages on the website. It was one example after another of burglar alarms, CCTV equipment, electronic alarm systems and well-dressed, muscular male security guards. She clicked on the 'About Us' page. There was a message in the form of a letter. It was in an italicised font.

Dear Householder, Beaufort Holdings aims to put your mind at rest on the issue of home security.
Every home and every homeowner is individual. Our security solutions are distinctive and personal.

Then there was an elaborate signature, the name printed in plain font underneath:
Margaret Spicer, Managing Director.
It was an interesting feminine touch to an otherwise male company. Rose saw that it was based in Chelsea – Brechin Place, SW7.

Rose closed it down. It was time she put the silver SUV out of her head. Joshua certainly had. He had put everything but Skeggsie out of his head. She opened the back door and called out to Poppy. The dog came running up the garden and bounced into the kitchen. Rose gave her some food from a tin.

She went upstairs and ran a bath. She needed a rest and her hair hadn't been washed for days. She had no idea what time Joshua was coming back but she wanted to make the most of the quiet and calm that was in the house. She put her phone on charge and saw that she had a couple of missed texts from Anna. She read them through and sent a short text back telling her that they were all right.

Then she went into the bathroom.

She was in the kitchen washing some plates when Joshua returned. He stood across the room from her. She noticed his jumper was fraying at the bottom.

'The police are looking for Sean Spenser,' he said.

She nodded, drying her hands.

'Also, I found out some stuff from Bob about the attack,' he said slowly.

Rose stared at him, sensing that he was going to say something awful.

'Skeggsie was robbed. He had no wallet or phone on him.'

She waited. What was next?

'And he lost a lot of blood. A lot.'

Rose remembered Joshua's coat, the bloodstain that seemed to eat up the fabric.

'Which means he didn't die straight away. He might have been conscious for a while.'

'How do they know that?'

'If the victim dies the heart stops so there's not much blood. But if the victim is *alive* the heart is still pumping the blood round the body so more blood is lost.'

'So he was just lying there. If only someone had found him sooner,' Rose said.

'I walked down Jesmond Road, past the alley on my way back to the pub. Maybe he was moaning then and I just didn't hear him.'

Joshua had the flat of his hand over the lower half of his face. His fingers gripped his jaw, his other hand fiddling with the bottom of his jumper. His eyes were steely and hard, staring straight ahead. He was like two people. One was in the grip of suppressed rage; the other was a damaged boy whose clothes were unravelling.

She walked across and leant against him. She pressed her face into his ribs so that she could hear the slow pounding of his heart.

'He bled to death,' he said. 'I could have saved him.'

'Ssh . . .'

She looked up at him. She put her fingers up to his mouth to stop him speaking. His face had a look of utter desolation. It filled her with emotion. She put her hand behind his head and touched his hair. Then she pulled him towards her.

'Rosie,' he said, holding back.

But she reached up and kissed him on the lips. He closed his eyes and let his mouth brush hers. She pushed herself against him and felt his arm go tightly round her back, pulling her closer to him as he kissed her harder. She clung on to him. His mouth was hot and his lips were dry. After a few moments he stopped.

She let her face rest against his neck.

He was burning up as if he had a fever.

'Rosie,' he said, 'I don't know what to do. I'm lost.'

Rose didn't answer. It wasn't the first time they'd both been lost.

TWENTY-ONE

When she woke the next morning Joshua was already up. The bed beside her was cold. She turned over and put her arm into the empty space where he had slept. She rubbed her face on his pillow and wondered where he was. She could hear no sounds from downstairs. She threw back the duvet. She was wearing Joshua's old pyjamas and socks. She stretched out her arms, yawning widely, looking round his room. On the bedside table she saw a piece of paper.

> *Rose, Got a text from Bob. The police found Sean Spenser in South Shields. They've got him at Farringdon Hall Police Station. Bob's going there so I thought I'd tag along. See what's happening. See you later. Josh x*

She got up and walked into the box room. She looked out of the window. It was a bright day. Looking at the cars Rose could see a layer of frost. Skeggsie's Mini was still parked outside so Bob must have picked Joshua up on his way to the station in South Shields.

She hugged herself.

Something was happening between her and Joshua.

The previous evening they'd sat sandwiched together on the sofa and watched one television programme after another until they were both dropping off to sleep. Joshua had taken her hand and pulled her up the stairs and when he got to his room he'd rummaged around in a drawer and thrown some pyjamas at her. He'd turned off the light before she was quite ready so she'd had to stumble towards the bed. Once under the duvet he'd kissed her over and over. He held her tightly so she was hardly moving. After a while he seemed exhausted with the kisses and fell back on to the pillow. They didn't speak but lay wrapped around each other. More than anything she'd wanted to ask him if *this* was what he really wanted. Or was it just grief pushing him towards her. She didn't say it, though. It was not the right time. Not while he was *hurting*.

Now Rose got dressed. She sorted out some of her clothes and decided to put them in the washing machine. At the same time she made some breakfast. Poppy followed her around the kitchen in the hope of scraps. The sun was shining in through the windows and the radio was playing music that she liked and for a few moments it seemed like an ordinary day – a day when there wasn't a great shadow hanging over her.

An ordinary day.

Could life ever be like that for her and Joshua?

Poppy wanted to go out so she opened the back door. The front doorbell rang. Timidly. For a moment Rose wasn't quite sure what she had heard. Then it rang again and she went out and opened it. A woman was standing there. She was wearing a long coat over a suit. She was carrying a briefcase and a carrier bag.

'Is Stuart Johnson's nephew in?'

'No, he's not. Can I help? I'm . . . family . . .'

'Look I'm . . . My name is Barbara Greaves and I am a friend of Stuart's. I wanted to say on behalf of my family how sorry we were to hear about his accident.'

'Why don't you come in?'

Rose held the door open. Barbara Greaves looked as if she wasn't sure but then she walked in.

'The kitchen's straight through,' Rose said and Barbara headed towards it. Her coat floated around her, almost coming to her ankles. In the kitchen she took it off and draped it over the back of a chair. Her carrier bag was on the seat and she put her hand in it and pulled out a large wrapped present. It sat on the table.

Rose thought of the name *Barbara Greaves*. It rang a bell.

'Can I get you a cup of tea?'

'No, thank you. I'm on my way to work so I won't stay long.'

There were scrabbling sounds on the door.

'It's the dog,' Rose explained.

'You can let it in. I like dogs.'

Rose opened the door and Poppy ran straight over to Barbara, her tail wagging furiously. Barbara sat down and began to *shush* Poppy and stroke her ears. After a few moments she pushed the gift towards Rose.

'My family and I, we bought this for Stuart. I think he'll like it – it's a book about vintage MGs. We were hoping his nephew would take it to him in hospital. I thought of going myself but it didn't seem quite right. I haven't seen him in a couple of years and I didn't want to just turn up . . .'

'That's very nice of you,' Rose said, still puzzled.

'I would have waited to come and see him when he's out of hospital but my family and I are just about to go off on a skiing holiday. I didn't want Stuart to think that we'd not thought of him at this difficult time.'

'I don't really understand. You and your family were close to Stuart?'

'He was my form teacher. He helped me and my parents through a really rough time. It was because of him that I eventually got to university. I won't say everything in our lives is fine now but it's a lot better than it used . . .'

'You're Judy Greave's sister,' Rose said, the name suddenly slotting into place.

Judy Greaves. The Butterfly Murder.

'Yes, I am. I don't know what you know about . . .'

'Stuart has some newspaper cuttings in a file. Joshua and I read them. It was a dreadful story . . .'

'It was a bad time.'

There was an awkward silence. Barbara's hand was resting on the gift, her fingers tapping. There was a label that said *To Stuart, from the Greaves family*. Rose remembered then that Judy Greaves had been sitting in a car in Morrisons' car park when she was abducted. Her mother had left her sister in charge of her but she had gone back into the shop and left Judy on her own. Barbara Greaves, the smart young woman sitting opposite her, had been that girl. As if reading her mind Barbara began to talk.

'My sister was ten and I was fourteen. My mum was always telling me to look after her. You have any sisters?'

Rose shook her head.

'Well, it's pretty annoying to be the older sister. *Barbara, will you see to Judy? Barbara, can you find Judy's school project? Barbara, can you stay in the car with Judy while I pop into Morrrisons?* You'll know the story of course. I didn't stay in the car and when I got back Judy had gone.'

Rose sat down at the table close to where Barbara was sitting. Poppy was lying on the floor.

'Even then I didn't call for help. I was probably in some daydream about a boy I liked or some such thing. Oh, this is silly. I don't even know you and I'm going on about this. It's been ten years. I should move on . . .'

'It's OK. Really . . .'

Barbara stood up and picked up her case. Her cheeks had reddened and Rose could see that she was upset. She hooked up her coat from the chair and gave a shaky smile.

'I must go,' she said.

Rose put a hand on her arm.

'I know what it's like to lose someone. My mother disappeared five years ago. I don't know where she is. I don't know what's happened to her and I think about her every day.'

Barbara stared at Rose. Her eyes glassed over and she seemed to slump back down into the seat.

'I'll make a cup of tea,' Rose said.

'Please, two sugars, no milk,' Barbara said.

Later when the tea had been drunk Barbara started to talk about it again.

'That afternoon when she disappeared was the worst afternoon of my life. At least I thought it was at the time. But then five days later when we got the phone call to say that they'd found her in that house, in that room . . .'

Rose stared down at the table.

'They said that they were all over the walls. Frame after frame of mounted butterflies. Someone said, one of the reporters I think, that there were maybe three or four hundred butterflies in that room. And Judy lying there . . .'

'I'm so sorry,' Rose said.

Barbara used one finger to push her mug away.

'Now I really must stop talking about it and go.'

Rose stood up. Barbara pointed at the gift.

'Tell Stuart there's a bottle of champagne on ice for him when he's on his feet again.'

Rose wondered what Barbara would say if she were to read Stuart's letter of confession. Maybe she wouldn't be shocked or saddened. Maybe she'd be even more grateful to him. When they got to the front door Barbara rested her case on the floor while she put her coat over her suit. Then she pulled a set of keys from her pocket and pointed them at a nearby car. Rose stood and waited for her to get in. When the car moved off she closed the front door.

Rose went up to Stuart's bedroom and opened his desk drawers one after the other. What was she looking for? Had Joshua filed away the Butterfly Murder papers? She shook her head. Looking at the shelves along the wall she saw the steel box that they'd found in the engine of the MG. She took it off the shelf and lifted the lid. All of Stuart's stuff was in it. She carried it to her room. She took the notebook and the letter and the newspaper cuttings out. Lying at the bottom was the Last Will and Testament envelope. She left that in the box and picked up the notebook, opening it at the first page.

The face of ten-year-old Judy Greaves looked back at her.

What had happened in Morrisons' car park? Had a man knocked on the window of the car that Judy was sitting in? Had he spun a story of some sort to get Judy to get out and follow him to his car? *Your mum asked me to come and get you. She slipped over in the shop and hurt her ankle. They're taking her to hospital now. I've got my car here and we can follow the ambulance.* Rose thought about the little girl looking out of the car window at the perfectly nice man who was offering to help her. Of course she would have gone. Rose would have gone. Any story that involved a mother would have overridden any advice on talking to strangers.

Poor Judy Greaves.

The front door sounded. Rose heard Joshua call out her name. She put the papers back in the steel box and pushed it under the bed.

'Hi!' she shouted.

There was no answer so she went downstairs, tense about what information Joshua would have about Rory Spenser's brother.

'Josh?'

She went into the kitchen and saw him sitting at the table, his face in a scowl.

'What's up?'

'Sean Spenser has an alibi. One of his mates' mothers says he was at her house. They're contacting her now.'

'Oh.'

'Bob thinks it might not hold. Once Sean has been interviewed a few times he might go back on it.'

'Did you see him? Sean, I mean?'

'No.'

'Give them time. He's bound to deny it.'

'That's what Bob says. What's this?'

Joshua pulled the wrapped book that Barbara Greaves had left.

'One of Stuart's old pupils came round. This is a gift . . .'

'For Stu?' Joshua said sharply.

Rose nodded. He tossed it aside.

'She was very nice. She was telling me that . . .'

'I can't be thinking about that now,' he said, standing up. 'I can't think about anything except this Skeggsie stuff, Rose. Not now. Don't bother me with it now.'

He walked out of the kitchen. Moments later she heard the front door slam. She stayed sitting at the table, her hand resting on the gift for Stuart.

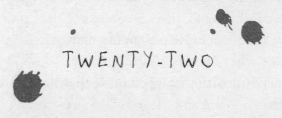

TWENTY-TWO

Rose went out in the afternoon and walked along the Promenade. She'd left Poppy at home so she could look in the shops. It was windy but not too cold and she liked the feel of the breeze ruffling her hair, blowing at her collar. She was tired of being in Stuart Johnson's house. She was tired of being here, in Newcastle. She wanted to go back to London. Everything was complicated. Joshua was so unhappy and there was nothing she could do about it. She ardently wished she could turn back time – the three of them in London, sitting eating in the kitchen at the flat in Camden, Joshua cooking, Skeggsie washing up, Rose drifting between the two.

What if she got a train home?

What if she went to the house now and wrote a letter for Joshua telling him that she had to go back and see Anna? What would he do? Maybe he would be better on his own; possibly she was a *burden* on top of all his other troubles.

Most of the shops were still shut for the Christmas holidays but a couple of cafes were open, the smell of bacon wafting temptingly from them. She passed the Lighthouse pub and then went along the front of the arcades, their machines pumping sounds like gunfire into the street.

She went into a charity shop. It was warm and there was music playing and she found herself looking through racks of women's clothes. She pulled out a black shirt that was her size. It was made from linen so it would crease but still she liked the shape of it. Next to it was a light yellow top, the colour subtle like misty sunshine. It wasn't her colour, but even so she took it to the till and paid for it. Outside the pavement was blocked by two elderly women standing talking, two shopping trolleys in between them. Rose moved past.

'Hello,' a voice said.

She looked round and saw Michelle Hinds coming towards her.

'Oh hi!' she said, holding her bag close to her chest as though she'd been caught doing something wrong.

'How are you guys?'

'Not so bad,' Rose lied.

Michelle was immaculately made-up, eyeliner on her lids and her lips painted pillar-box red. Her coat was open and showed a low cut top over black trousers.

'I'm glad I met you. There's something I wanted to talk

to you about. I'm on my way to work,' Michelle said. 'Will you walk with me?'

'Sure.'

They carried on, weaving in and out of passers-by. Michelle talked as she went, Rose straining to hear some of the things she said.

'I wanted to tell Joshua the other night but I didn't want him rushing off and being aggressive with Rory Spenser. Now I'm thinking you might be a better person to tell just so Josh knows I've been straight with him.'

'What is it?'

'When I said I was with Rory in the Beer Hut I was being honest but he did go out for about fifteen minutes. He went to get some dope. To take back to the party.'

'So he was on his own for a while?'

'It was about eleven twenty, something like that? I didn't mention it to the policeman who I spoke to because I didn't want to get Rory into trouble. He's already got a couple of cautions for possession.'

'But if he was on his own for fifteen minutes he could have gone to that alley?' Rose said.

'He went out for dope. He came back with some dope. I'm not telling you this so that you can start thinking that he killed Josh's friend. I'm just trying to be honest with Josh. I can see he is in a state.'

Rose nodded.

'Rory didn't kill his friend.'

They were in front of the Royal.

'Look, he does boxing now and on top of that he's got an interview for a college course in a couple of weeks. He's not the idiot he comes across. He talks before he thinks and he doesn't like Josh-u-a. But he's harmless. Why don't you go and talk to him? He lives in Cork Street, about a mile down Jesmond Road on the right. Number Six. He's a pain but he wouldn't kill anyone.'

She looked at Rose. Rose didn't know what to say.

'I've got to go. I'm due to start in five minutes. I'm on my knees I've worked so much this week.'

'Thanks, Michelle,' Rose said.

'You're quite nice, pet. For a southerner.'

Just then the front doors of the hotel opened and some people came out. One of them was the blonde woman with the dog. She was fussing over the dog and pulling car keys out of a bag. Rose stepped back away from the entrance to the car park. She beckoned for Michelle to move with her.

'I'm due in work,' Michelle said.

'Could you find out who that woman is? She's been staying in your hotel.'

'Which one?' Michelle said, looking round.

'The blonde woman with the dog.'

'Oh, her. She's Mrs Spicer. Everyone knows who she is because of the dog. She's from London but has family here and has come up for Christmas. She's a nice lady. And the dog's name is Alfie. Anything else?'

'No,' she said.

Margaret Spicer, the Managing Director of Beaufort Holdings.

'Bye,' Michelle sang out the word and ran off through the car park and into the hotel.

When Rose got back to the house she saw the leather jacket hanging on the hall pegs. Joshua was back from wherever he had gone. She wondered if she should tell him what Michelle had said about Rory. It might make matters worse, though. He might rush round to Rory's and there could be another fight. Wouldn't it be better to leave the whole thing to the police? Skeggsie was the son of a retired police officer. They would do everything they could to find who was responsible. No doubt they would find out about Rory's trip to buy dope from someone else.

She walked upstairs. Joshua's room door was ajar. He was lying on his bed. He got up as she passed and followed her to the box room.

'I've been thinking,' he said, as though he was continuing a conversation that they'd been having, as though he hadn't been sharp with her and stormed out of the house. 'I've been going back over Christmas Eve.'

Rose nodded. He leant on the windowsill. Outside it was beginning to get dark.

'The walk from the pub to the alley in Jesmond Road where Skeggsie got killed took about ten minutes?'

'Sounds about right.'

'Do you remember much about that walk?'

Rose thought for a moment.

'Because I don't,' Joshua went on. 'Finding Skeggsie, in that alley, was so huge that it obliterated everything else that night for me. When I gave a statement I think I just started from when we walked past the alley, when you heard a noise.'

'I remember soon after we walked out of the pub we passed a group of people.'

'I vaguely do. But the point is the *rest* of that walk, I don't remember it at all.'

'Why is it important?'

'Because we passed people coming from that direction. One of them might have seen something. Or we might have seen something significant that at the time we didn't think anything of.'

'I don't see how we can help that now, four days later.'

'We could do a reconstruction. We could wait until it's dark and do the walk again.'

'What for?'

'To jog our memories. We do the walk, try and visualise what it was like on Christmas Eve. It may trigger things that we have forgotten about.'

Rose was frowning. She glanced at the window. It

wouldn't be long before it was properly dark. Would it hurt to walk from the Lighthouse to the alley on Jesmond Road? She wondered then about Rory Spenser. How long would it have taken for him to walk from the Beer Hut to that same alley?

'What do you think?'

'OK,' she said. 'Let's go this evening. About ten when the pub will be fullish. That way it will seem more like it was on Christmas Eve.'

'Good,' he said. 'It's important to be *doing* something.'

She nodded. Maybe after they'd done that they could go along to the Beer Hut. Just for a drink. And to time the walk.

At just after ten they walked into the Lighthouse. It was full, loud music playing from a group on the stage, people standing watching. There was barely enough room to get to the bar.

'OK,' Joshua said. 'We were standing here. You went and got some beers while I rang Skeggs. We drank the beers. And then we decided to go and walk back to my house to see if we could catch Skeggs. We left the pub.'

Rose pushed the pub door open and stepped out into the cold night air. The street seemed busy. A cab was pulling up and letting a group of girls out. This was different to Christmas Eve. It had been snowing, she remembered, and there had been no cab. Now they walked along the Promenade. There were a group of boys standing round smoking and drinking from bottles. They were laughing loudly, taking up a lot of the pavement space. Joshua had to say, 'Excuse us' for them to get through.

'This was where we passed the people. They'd just turned out of Jesmond Road and were heading in our direction. It was a big group of young people.'

'No,' Rose said. 'There were two groups. Some people in front and couple of girls singing together further behind.'

'But they all came round the corner.'

'Yes.'

They turned the corner and began to walk along Jesmond Road.

'Cab place is full,' Joshua said. 'People getting taxis into Newcastle centre for the clubs. Same as Christmas Eve.'

'Fish and chip shop open.'

The lighting dimmed as they moved further along Jesmond Road.

'I'm trying to think if there was anyone in this area that night. A passer-by, someone getting out of a car. A couple talking on a corner. Anyone we might have seen and not registered.'

Rose looked up and down the dark street. There were boarded up shops and a long line of cars parked by the pavement. There were advertising hoardings and a pedestrian crossing. Had there been anyone on the crossing that night?

She sighed. There was something at the back of her head. Something she was trying to remember. They'd almost reached the alley and Joshua was slowing down. He stopped completely and leant back against the wall.

'This is a waste of time.'

He had his hands in his pockets. She looked round, her eyes scouring the shopfronts, the houses, the cars. She saw a bus stop. Could that be significant? Had a bus come along and let someone off at that spot? Had she and Joshua been too wrapped up in their talk to even notice?

She turned back to him. He was so easily discouraged. What had happened to all his energy and passion? He looked tired. Her heart felt sore at the sight of him. She moved towards him, stood in front of him.

'It was a good idea,' she said, standing close to him. 'It may jog a memory later.'

He was staring at her. His eyes were heavy and she felt herself being drawn towards him. His hands were by his side. They weren't touching, yet it was as if she was being pulled to him by something she couldn't stop. She stepped closer and put the side of her face on the cold leather of his jacket.

Then it came to her.

Someone else turned on to the Promenade on Christmas Eve.

'The homeless man!' she said, standing back from him.

He looked around, a puzzled expression on his face.

'When we were turning the corner from the Promenade to Jesmond Road I saw a homeless man walk round. Just after the two girls who were singing. I remember now.'

'How do you know he was homeless?'

'Because I'd seen him earlier, over there, when I was going to the pub. I gave him some money. Maybe he was there all evening. Standing just down from the cab place where there were more people.'

'He might have been there all the time.'

'He may have seen something.'

'How do we find him? Why isn't he here tonight?'

'Maybe he stands in different spots. I don't know. Why don't we ask in the cab office?'

Joshua strode off. Rose followed. In moments they were in the yellow light of the cab office. They edged past the queue of waiting people. It was the second time they'd done it and Rose kept apologising. 'We're not here for a cab, sorry.' It was the same woman at the desk as before. This time she had silver baubles on her ears, just like those on any Christmas tree.

'Excuse me, do you know the name of the homeless man who is sometimes along from your shop?' Joshua said.

'Why, you want to send him a card?'

'No, I . . . Why would I want to send him a card?'

'He's in hospital.'

'Why?'

'Pneumonia, I heard. Why do these people stay out when there are perfectly good hostels? It's stupid if you ask me.'

'Do you know his name?'

'George something,' she said.

A voice from behind spoke.

'George Dudek. He's Polish. I heard he collapsed on the Promenade on Christmas Day.'

Rose turned round to see who was speaking. A young man with his arm around a girl.

'What hospital is he in?' Joshua said.

'Royal Victoria.'

'Thanks.'

They walked out of the cab place.

'What are you going to do?'

'I'll contact Bob. He and I could go and see this guy first thing in the morning.'

'Why not just tell the police?'

'It might come to nothing and I don't want to distract them from following up Sean Spenser's alibi.'

Joshua was smiling. Rose was pleased. She'd remembered something that might be important. She looked across the road at the boarded up shops where the alley was. The cab office was no more than a minute or so away.

'I'd like a drink,' she said. 'Let's go to that other pub, the Beer Hut.'

'If you want.'

They walked off, Rose glancing at the time on her mobile as they went.

TWENTY-THREE

Joshua went out early and Rose took her time getting dressed. She was thoughtful. The previous night's walk from the cab firm to the Beer Hut had taken four minutes. That meant that Rory Spenser had plenty of time to get to the alley and back. Maybe the search to buy dope was a ruse. Possibly he already had the dope in his pocket and it was just an excuse to go out. When he got back to the pub he simply showed Michelle what he had and she assumed he'd been buying dope. Or maybe not.

She hadn't mentioned it to Joshua. He had been fired up about finding George Dudek, the homeless man. Bob and he were going to the Royal Victoria hospital. Mentioning it would have only confused matters. Maybe the homeless man had seen something. Possibly he had seen someone like Rory follow Skeggsie and pull him into the alley.

Was it likely?

The day stretched ahead of her. It was Saturday. She'd

been in Newcastle for over a week. In three days' time it was New Year's Day. What would the New Year bring for her and Joshua? More of the same or some kind of fresh start? She wandered around upstairs, in and out of the bathroom, wondering whether to wash her hair again. In the box room she saw the corner of the metal box that she'd shoved under the bed. It held all the details of the Butterfly Murder. She remembered then that Skeggsie had brought the notebooks paraphernalia up to Newcastle in a small brown suitcase. His dad's house had a good alarm system, he'd said, so it was safe. It was just Skeggsie who hadn't been safe.

When they got back to London they should open a safety deposit box, he'd suggested. Would they do that now?

Rose pictured the trip back to London, Joshua driving the Mini, her sitting in the passenger seat. Would they talk? Play music? Sit in silence thinking about why there were only two of them in the car? And when they arrived at the flat in London they would have to unlock the various Chubb locks that Skeggsie had had installed. They would go up the stairs and walk into the long kitchen with its narrow table. Everything would be tidy and clean because that had been important to Skeggsie. Every dish had its place on the shelves, every cooking implement had its section of the cupboard.

And Skeggsie's bedroom and study. Would Josh leave it as it was or would there come a time when Skeggsie's things would be packed in brown cardboard boxes, like his Christmas presents, and sent back to Newcastle to Bob?

The house phone rang. The sound startled Rose because she hadn't heard it before. She picked up the receiver. A male voice spoke.

'Is that Rose? It's Stuart here.'

It was Stuart Johnson, the man she'd been talking about for days.

'Hello!' she said. 'How are you? I was going to come and see you but with everything that happened . . .'

'That's fine, lass. Really I understand what an awful week it's been.'

'Are you feeling better?'

'Not too bad. My leg is in plaster but I can just about hobble round. I'm ringing really to let you know that the hospital are going to let me out on Monday morning. New Year's Eve. I've told Joshua but he's a bit distracted and I thought I'd let you know as well. You don't have to make any preparations but Joshua will need to organise a taxi to pick me up. They'll discharge me after ten. Then we'll meet at last.'

'That'll be nice.'

'Goodbye, lass.'

Rose replaced the telephone. Stuart was coming home.

Maybe that would be a good time for her to go back to London.

She ruffled her hair with her hands. She couldn't just hang around the house all day – she had to *do* something. She went downstairs and put her coat on and picked up her phone. Poppy looked hopefully at her but she shook her head.

Cork Street was off Jesmond Road, as Michelle had described. The houses were sandwiched tightly together and didn't have front gardens. Rose walked up to Number Six, sidestepped two large wheelie bins and knocked on the door. Moments later it was opened by a small girl in pyjamas.

'Is Rory in?' Rose said, smiling at her.

A woman appeared. Without a word to Rose she called out Rory's name and pulled the little girl away from the door. There was the sound of heavy footsteps stomping down the stairs and Rose saw Rory coming towards her.

'What?' he said, his face taking on a dark look, his eyes going behind her, looking out on to the street.

'I'm on my own,' she said. 'I just want to talk to you.'

'What about?' he said, half hidden behind the front door.

'Is there somewhere we could go? A cafe?'

He looked as though he was thinking it through. Rose gave an exaggerated sigh.

'Michelle Hinds said I should come and see you. To talk about the fifteen minutes you were out of the pub on Christmas Eve.'

He looked at her with a sullen expression. Then he took his phone out of his pocket and began a text. He never said a word and she felt stupid standing there. He sent the text and continued staring at her. Then she realised he was waiting for an answer. A beep sounded and he glanced down at his phone. She guessed he was contacting Michelle.

'There's a cafe round the corner,' he said.

He pulled a coat from behind the door and came out of the house and walked in front of her. He didn't speak but led her to a cafe with steamed-up windows.

'You want a tea, coffee?' she said, getting some money out.

'Coffee,' he said.

She got the drinks and went and joined him at a table near the window. Beside them was a group of older men, playing cards.

'Michelle said you left the pub for fifteen minutes?'

'She tell the police?'

'She didn't want to get you into trouble. Because of the dope.'

'Why'd she tell you?'

'She wanted Josh to know. She wanted to be honest with him but she was afraid he would come round here and make trouble. So she told me instead.'

He shrugged. He took his phone out of his pocket and stared down at the screen. She blew through her teeth.

'Sorry, I wasted your time. I'll pass it on to the police then they can deal with it,' she said, moving her chair back as if to stand up.

'No need to go off on one.'

He laid his phone down on the table by the side of his drink.

'I just don't get it, see? Joshua hates you for the way you treated Skeggs when he was at school. But Martin, who also knows what you were like then, sticks up for you. Why are they on different sides here?'

Rory drank his coffee and mumbled something.

'Pardon?' Rose said.

'Because I'm not like that any more. I don't hit out at people no more. I go boxing. You have to learn to control your aggression.'

'You were verbally aggressive when I saw you in the pub.'

'That's just talk.'

'But that's how trouble starts.'

'I don't get in trouble now but Johnson comes back from London and starts throwing his weight around. Darren Skeggs looks like he's ready to jump out of his skin. The words just come out. But I don't hit anyone any more. That's all in the past. I paid my price for it. You ask Johnson and he'll tell you. Him and Marty both gave me a good kicking.'

Rose didn't speak. It made her feel slightly sick to think of it.

'They'll tell you I deserved it. Maybe I did.'

'Was it that that made you change? That *kicking*?'

'No. Marty came back from York one weekend and took me to boxing. That's all. That's what did it.'

'What? The boxing?'

'No! It was the fact that Marty, who hated my guts when we were at school, took me to boxing. He took the time and he came with me and he got me started. I told him I'd never hit anyone else again unless it was self-defence and I can't let him down. I didn't say I wouldn't rile anyone or cheek anyone or give abuse. All I said was that I wouldn't hit anyone and I haven't.'

Rose stared at this white-faced, overweight boy. She was suddenly sure that he was telling the truth.

Her phone beeped. She looked at the screen. **George Dudek left hospital two days ago. He's at a hostel in Gateshead. Bob and I are going there. See you later. Josh.**

'That Johnson?'

She nodded.

'He upset about his uncle and then Darren Skeggs?'

'Of course. His uncle is like his dad. Skeggsie was his best friend for years. Of course he's upset!'

Rory nodded.

'I never did nothing to Darren Skeggs.'

'What about your brother?'

'Honestly, I couldn't say. He's capable. Whether he's that bothered I don't know.'

The game of cards had finished on the next table and one man was laughing loudly. The others were tapping the side of their cups with spoons. Rose supposed that he had to buy another round of teas for winning.

'I should go,' she said.

'I saw Johnson's uncle around. I didn't know him to speak to but I knew who he was. My mum worked in his school as a dinner lady. Well, they call them lunchtime supervisors now.'

Rose looked at her phone. It was before eleven. She had no idea where Gateshead was but she was sure that Joshua would be away for hours.

'And I saw him there, on the cliff, on the night he fell.'

'What?'

'I mean I didn't *see* him fall over. Obviously if I'd seen him go over I would have done something about it. Just because I don't get on with Johnson doesn't mean I would ignore someone going over the cliff.'

'What did you see?'

'I saw him walking with his dog. I passed him on the cliff path. I was heading for the old cafe. Some mates were going there for a smoke.'

'Why didn't you tell this to the police?'

'I don't talk to the police unless I have to. Anyway, he was all right, wasn't he?'

'Then what?'

'Then nothing. I had a smoke with my mates. I never

saw him again. After a couple of hours or so I walked back along the cliff path. If I'd known he was down there . . .'

'No one saw him till the morning.'

Rose pictured Stuart lying on the ledge while people walked past on the cliff above – in the same way people had walked past the alleyway where Skeggsie had lain.

Rory was still talking.

'I walked back along the path about half eleven. It was deserted.'

Rose nodded.

'Except for the woman with the hair up on top, in a ponytail.'

'Woman?'

'I was watching where I was going. Looking down at the ground. I'd had a bit of dope and I was out of it. When I looked up I saw her standing on the path ahead of me. Maybe ten metres away? She was looking round. When she saw me coming she walked off.'

'Looking round?'

'Yes. The funny thing was when she went off I could hear the scraping of her heels on the path. No one walks the cliff path in high heels.'

'What time was this?'

'About eleven thirty, maybe later, maybe twelve.'

'But you saw Stuart much earlier.'

'Yeah, nine? Ten? Not sure.'

Rose stood up. The card players from the next table looked at her.

'I have to go.'

'You're not going to tell the police about the dope?'

'No.'

'What about Johnson?'

Rose was walking out of the cafe. Rory was following alongside her.

'Why do you always call Joshua by his surname?'

'That's what we do. Boys' school.'

'But you called Skeggsie by his first name. A name that none of his friends ever used.'

'I wasn't his friend. He made that clear. His dad arrested my brother and Darren didn't want to know him nor me. Are you going to tell Johnson about me being out of the pub?'

'At some point I will. He's still too upset. He's not thinking straight. Where's Morrisons? Is it near?'

'What?'

'The supermarket? Morrisons.'

'By the golf course.'

'Can I walk there from here?'

'Yeah. Keep going down Jesmond Road till you get to the lights by the funeral parlour. Turn right and carry on. Then I think it's a left turn. Twenty minutes or so?'

'Thanks.'

Rose walked away from Rory. She headed quickly

along the pavement. When she got to the lights by the undertakers she looked round and saw that he was standing in the exact same place. As if he had nowhere else to go.

TWENTY-FOUR

Morrisons was easy to find. She passed a small park and then turned on to a road of shops that led up to the supermarket. She'd remembered that Susie Tyler worked in Morrisons. She was keen to see her because she was sure that it was Susie Rory had seen on the cliff path. She had no idea whether Susie would be working today but she didn't know where she lived and she didn't have anything else to do so she decided it was a worthwhile trip.

She walked towards the pharmacy section but couldn't see Susie Tyler on the counter. She waited while a couple of people were served and then asked the assistant when Susie Tyler was on duty. She was told that she would be on in an hour.

An hour wasn't so long to wait.

She bought a sandwich and a drink and paid at the self-service till. Then she wandered back out of the shop and headed for the park that she had passed. Although it was cold she didn't feel like sitting in the shop eating her food.

The park was tiny and she sat on a bench by the gate. In the middle was a small play area, a couple of swings and tiny metal horses on springs. A woman was sitting at a picnic table, watching two children on the swings. She was saying, 'Careful now, not too high!' and they were shouting, 'Look, Mummy, look!'

Rose wondered what it would be like for a couple not to be able to have children. It had almost finished Susie and Greg Tyler's marriage but they had got back together. She remembered them coming out of the shopping centre with their Mothercare bags.

Why had they got back together?

She finished her sandwich and put the wrapper in the bin. The park had a sign, *Primrose Park*. The road curved around it and when she looked up at the adjacent houses she saw the street sign, *Primrose Crescent*.

It rang a bell with her and in a second she remembered it.

The house where Judy Greaves's body had been found was in Primrose Crescent. It was mentioned in the notebook that Stuart Johnson had sent to Brendan years before telling him about the Butterfly Murder. It was Number Six, she remembered. She stood for a moment and looked along the houses. They were big, mostly semi-detached. She was standing opposite Number Twenty-eight, the numbers in descending order. She walked along, gathering speed as she went. She was curious to see the house in which this terrible thing had happened. When she reached the house she stood still in front of it. Three storeys high, it was brick-built, Victorian, maybe. The front had a mass of creeping ivy. She glanced down at the front door. There were three separate bells. It had been turned into flats. The front garden was paved over and there were bike rests and wheelie bins vying for space. The ground floor had wooden shutters on the windows as if no one was up yet or perhaps the residents were away for Christmas. The ivy was creeping across the glass in places.

Rose wondered if that was where Judy Greaves had been found. In her head she saw the frames of mounted butterflies hung on the walls. All stiff and dead, a single pin through each one fixing it on to a board. It made her shiver to think of the girl lying in the midst of this flamboyant exhibition. She pushed up her sleeve and looked at her butterfly, the tattoo she'd had done months before. Other people had done the same thing: her mother, Kathy, and Joshua's father, Brendan. But her butterfly was beautiful because it was an image of a live insect not the carcass of a dead one.

She looked up at the building. The awful discovery could have been in any of the other rooms. Beside the front door, to the right, there was something that had been swallowed up by the ivy. She looked around the street aware of how odd she must seem. Then she walked up the short garden path and reached up, pulling at the ivy, feeling its powerful hold. She tried to curl it back across what she could see was a wooden nameplate. She used both hands and edged the ivy far enough off to see the words. *Beaufort House.*

The front door swung open.

A man stood there, staring at her.

'What do you want?'

'Sorry . . . I . . .'

'The names of the people living here are on the bells. What are you doing?'

Rose saw that she had three or four tendrils of ivy in her hand.

'Wrong house, sorry . . .' she said, smiling apologetically.

She backed away, dropping the ivy behind her. The front door made a mighty slam and she flinched but kept walking without looking back. As she rounded the periphery of the park play area she almost knocked into a post with a gold coloured plaque. Startled, she stopped for a second and read the sign. *This play and rest area is dedicated to the memory of Judy Greaves whose life was cut short in tragic circumstances. May the sound of children's laughter for ever ring loudly. RIP 1992–2002*

Rose stared at the notice. Then she looked around the quiet street with its pretty houses. The two children were still flying back and forth on the swings. The mother was smiling at them.

She walked away slowly, thoughtful.

The house that Judy Greaves's body was found in was called Beaufort House. It had the same name as the company which owned the silver SUV.

In Morrisons she stood along from the pharmacy counter.

Susie Tyler appeared soon after.

Rose walked up to the counter and Susie turned round to serve her. For once her hair was not in a ponytail but tied at the nape of her neck. She was wearing a badge on her chest, the kind that came with a greetings card. This one said *Mummy-To-Be*.

'Congratulations,' Rose said. 'It must be great for you and Greg to be having a baby after such a long time of trying.'

Susie looked more closely at Rose.

'I'm sorry, do I know you?'

'I'm Joshua's . . . I was at Joshua Johnson's house when you called last Friday.'

'Oh.'

'Is there somewhere we could talk?'

'I'm at work now.'

'Later. Tea break or something?'

'I'm sorry but I don't know you . . .'

'I wanted to ask you why you went up to Cullercoats on the night that Stuart Johnson fell.'

'What?'

'Someone saw you. About eleven thirty?'

Rose stared at her. Susie looked as if she didn't know whether to get angry or upset.

'How is Stuart?'

'Ok, I think.'

'Maybe I could slip out, get my friend to cover for me. Fifteen minutes? There are some benches in the car park.'

'OK.'

Rose found the benches. She sat down and got her phone out and saw that she had a message. **We're at the hostel in Gateshead. George Dudek is out!!!! We're going to wait for him for an hour then give up. See you about two-ish?**

Would the homeless man have any information for them or would it be another dead end? Could it just be as Bob was hinting at the other night, a random robbery and murder?

Greg Tyler appeared with Susie.

She must have called him the moment Rose left the pharmacy. They were walking across the car park towards her. When they got to her Rose didn't speak. She just looked from one to the other. Susie sat down on the bench but Greg stayed standing.

'You don't have to say a word to this girl,' Greg said to his wife.

Susie shrugged. 'We haven't done anything wrong.'

Rose noticed that she'd taken her badge off.

'Are you pregnant?'

Susie nodded. Rose waited. A question hung in the air between them.

'It's Stuart's baby.'

'For God's sake!' Greg hissed, looking round. 'Don't tell all our business out here in the car park! Come and sit in the car at least.'

Rose followed them until they got to a black car.

'You get in the back,' Greg said, hooking his thumb at Rose.

Rose got in, stifling a response. It was as if she was the one being questioned, not the other way round. Susie turned her face to Rose between the two front seats. Greg stared straight ahead.

'Greg and me can't have kids. I told you that last week. That's why things went bad between us and I ended up having the affair with Stuart. But that's in the past . . .'

Greg's hand reached across to Susie.

'I found out I was pregnant and I ended it with Stuart and I stupidly told him about the baby. He was adamant that we should stay together. He became really angry. That's why Greg and him had a fight here in the car park. I told him I was going to have the baby and that Greg and me would bring it up as our own but he didn't want that. He said he would take me to court and try to get joint custody. It was a mess!'

Susie was agitated. Her voice was cracking.

'Don't, Suse . . .'

'You tell her then! You know more about it than me!'

Greg turned round. He didn't make eye contact with Rose but looked down at the side of his seat, rubbing the fabric.

'I told him to keep away from Susie. I told him he could go to court if he liked – the baby would still be with us. Then, on the Wednesday, he rang me at work and said he wanted to meet up Cullercoats. He said he wanted to sort it all once and for all. I got there early and I waited in the car and then, like I said to you before, I got angry. I got out and walked around trying to calm down. Then I see him arguing with this guy further up the cliff path. The guy walks off and then Johnson follows him. I wait. I'm about to give up, go back to my car, when he comes back. I can tell he's riled up by the row he's already had and he's drunk. His dog's running around like it's some game. He comes straight at me and he says, *The world would be a better place if you were out of it!* And he grabs hold of my arm and starts to pull me towards the cliff edge. All the while he's mumbling about *Some people don't deserve to live!* It was ridiculous. I shook him off and he looked at me like he'd actually been serious about throwing me off the cliff. I just laughed at him and he made this dismissive gesture. He threw one hand up to wave me off as if I was nothing. It must have unbalanced him and he stumbled backwards and I walked away. I didn't think it was enough for him to fall over. I had no idea how close to the cliff edge he was. No idea.'

'You weren't even sure he'd fallen off,' Susie said.

'At first I thought he'd just stumbled and I walked off but then I remembered he was drunk and I didn't want him to lie out in the cold all night so I went back and looked for him. His dog was still there but he wasn't. Anywhere. That was when I realised that he must have gone over. I called out, two, three times. Honestly, I called out but there was no answer and I just panicked.'

'I was all for ringing the police, the ambulance, the coastguard but . . .'

'I told her not to. I said I was sure he was dead. I don't know those cliffs that well, especially not in the dark, but I thought the fall would have killed him.'

'But you went back there later,' Rose said to Susie.

'I wanted to be sure that there was nothing we could do. I found Poppy. She was just sitting a few metres away from the cliff path so I went and looked over. I called out again and again but there was no answer. I didn't see him.'

'You could have rung the emergency services.'

'Who would have believed me?' Greg said. 'I'd had a fight with the guy just over a week before. She's carrying his baby. Who would have believed me? I thought he was dead.'

It was hot in the car. Rose got out and stood by the side of it. Susie got out. Greg stayed in the driver's seat.

'I wanted to call an ambulance. That's why I went back. If there'd been any sign of life I'd have called the emergency services.'

'You didn't, though.'

'And I regret it. What are you going to do?'

Rose stretched her arms out. She was stiff and uncomfortable. Why should it be up to her to *do* anything? Why couldn't people clear up their own mess?

'You left the dog there. All night in the bitter cold.'

'I did think of taking the dog back with me but . . .'

'It would have mucked up your story. So you waited till the morning, until your neighbour told you about it then you went and picked up the dog.'

'Are you going to tell the police?'

'I'm not going to do anything. You and your husband are going to go to the police and make a new statement and tell the truth. This way you both look like decent people who made bad decisions.'

'We'll be prosecuted.'

'Maybe. Stuart's coming out of the hospital on New Year's Eve. So far he says he doesn't remember anything. That might be true. I don't know. The other possibility is that he knows and he's just not saying anything, he's keeping the information back to use in the future. If you go to the police you get it all out in the open now. You've got a baby on the way. It's up to you.'

Rose walked off. She didn't look behind. In her head

she heard Stuart's words to Greg Tyler – *The world would be a better place if you were out of it.* She remembered the letter he'd written to his solicitor, part of his Last Will and Testament. *I alone am guilty of the murder of Simon Lister.* Joshua's uncle had a dark side.

But then so did his father.

And her mother.

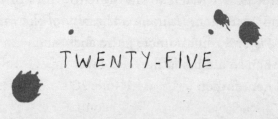

TWENTY-FIVE

Rose took a long slow walk back to the house.

She was trying to take in what Greg and Susie Tyler had told her.

It was an odd thing to do, to run away when someone was hurt. Human nature was to try and help. How could Greg simply turn his back? He could have at least phoned for an ambulance or the coastguard. If Stuart was dead the difficult situation was suddenly resolved for him. Susie and he would be able to bring up the new baby without any interference if Stuart wasn't around. Had that gone through Greg's mind?

Susie had gone back to the cliff later, though.

Had she been overcome with guilt?

Rose realised she had taken a different route. She was at a crossroads which she didn't recognise. Had she unconsciously avoided retracing her steps through Primrose Crescent?

She saw a sign for the *Seafront* and followed it.

* * *

Later she stood at the kitchen table and looked at what was in front of her. The grey steel box was empty and all of Stuart Johnson's papers relating to the Butterfly Murder were laid out on the surface. The notebook was at one end with Stuart's narrative of the abduction and murder of Judy Greaves. Also in the books were articles about the murder spaced over a year from June 2002 until September 2003 when Simon Lister was acquitted of the murder. Beside it was the pile of loose newspaper clippings that referred to the murder of Simon Lister on 23rd August 2004. Next to that was the letter from Brendan telling him that he wouldn't be able to help him but that he could come up for a visit on the weekend of 23rd and 24th August 2004. Stuart's confessional letter to his solicitor had been put back into the envelope containing his Last Will and Testament.

This was everything they had about the Butterfly Murder.

In the remaining space was Rose's laptop. Skeggsie's was on the work surface behind her.

Now she had found out that the house in which Judy Greaves's body had been discovered was called Beaufort House – the same name as the company that owned the silver SUV, the car that was driven by the woman with the white-blonde hair. The car that Rose had thought was following them. The driver's name was Margaret Spicer and she was one of the company directors – and *she* was currently staying at the Royal Hotel.

Stuart Johnson had been deeply involved in this case and had tried to persuade his brother to help. Rose sat down at the table and clicked on the saved file for Beaufort Holdings. She looked through the pages again and saw the name **Margaret Spicer, Company Director.**

Rose opened up a fresh Google search. She typed in *Margaret Spicer*. Some irrelevant articles came up about an actress called Margaret Spicer and a writer of historical fiction. Rose scrolled down. There were some mentions of Beaufort Holdings, mainly the pages she had already looked at. She opened a new search. She put the words *Margaret Spicer* and *Butterfly Murder* in together.

Pages of articles came up about the Butterfly Murder but none appeared to be linked with the name Margaret Spicer. She typed in *Margaret Spicer Simon Lister*. More pages came up with the words **Simon Lister** highlighted.

She sat back. Was there any point to this? Wasn't it just coincidental that the company was called Beaufort Holdings?

She opened up another search. She put *Primrose Crescent Margaret Spicer*. At the top of the list was an article from the local paper, the *Whitley Chronicle*. She sat up, excited. The words **Margaret Spicer** and **Primrose** were in bold. She double-clicked on the link. The newspaper article came up. She looked at the date – 15th June 2006. It was exactly four years after Judy Greaves's body was found. The headline was muted, none of the splash of the Butterfly

Murder press that there had been earlier. There was also a photograph of a group of three women holding small posies of flowers rather like plain clothes bridesmaids.

Memorial Park Opens for Judy

Primrose Crescent was the setting for the opening of a pretty park for local children to play in. The park, funded by the local authority, was built to commemorate ten-year-old Judy Greaves whose body was found in a nearby house in 2002. Judy's family asked for this to be a quiet and dignified affair. Local people attended and the park was officially opened by Judy's mother, Joanne Greaves, her sister Barbara Greaves and Margaret Spicer, the first police officer to discover Judy's body.

The article ended there. Rose stopped reading. She sat back. Margaret Spicer had been the first police officer to attend the body in the room full of butterflies. Rose looked at the photograph. It was tiny. Underneath it the caption read *Joanne Greaves (centre) stands with her daughter, Barbara, and WPC Spicer*. Rose could just about make out the likeness of Barbara Greaves, the girl who had visited her the day before. The other two faces were blurred. The woman on the right was Margaret Spicer.

Was it the *same* Margaret Spicer? The woman with the white-blonde hair?

Why hadn't her name been in any of the general press stories about the death? But Rose knew the answer to this. She was a WPC, a uniformed officer, anonymous, someone who just did their job. These people were never named in the papers. She's named here because she's been part of the healing process, the construction and opening of the children's park.

Was it Margaret Spicer of Beaufort Holdings?

She stared at the photograph. She couldn't stop the thought that Skeggsie could have enlarged the picture. She opened up her email and clicked on Eddie's address.

Eddie, are you online now? I need some help with one of Skeggsie's programmes. If you ring me I'd be so grateful.

She added her mobile number and waited. She noticed that it was almost three o'clock and Joshua was still out. He'd been gone most of the day. What would he say if he came in and saw the table covered with all this stuff?

Her mobile rang. She answered it.

'Hi, Rose. Eddie,' he said in a clipped voice.

'Eddie, thank you for calling me. I need a huge favour. It's something that Skeggsie used to do.'

'Yep. Fire away.'

'You sure you're not too busy? Or with family or something?'

'Rose. Tell me. Get to the point!'

Rose flinched at his tone but kept going.

'Skeggsie had a programme for enlarging photos, almost down to pixels. He said he used to use it for analysing brushstrokes in paintings.'

'Yep. Know it.'

'I have a small photograph of three women from a newspaper article. I'd like to enlarge one of the faces.'

'Yep. Can do. Email the links to me and I'll check it.'

'Will you have to go to the flat? To Skeggsie's computer?'

'Rose. This is the age of the internet. Skeggsie passed the programme on to me. Send me the link and I'll get back to you ASAP.'

The line went dead. Rose wrote the email and put the link to the newspaper article. She told Eddie she wanted the face on the right enlarged. She pressed *Send*. Then she pulled Skeggsie's laptop over. Her body felt tight and stiff, her shoulders rounded in concentration.

What was she thinking? That Margaret Spicer of Beaufort Holdings had been a WPC at one time and that she had been on duty when the body of Judy Greaves was discovered by an estate agent? That she now ran a security company and owned the silver SUV that had been following them?

She thought back to the times she had seen the car. It had been parked in the street, the woman and her dog sitting in it. Three times she'd seen it and then she'd looked for the registration number in Joshua's book. She found the number there, from the time when they stopped at the services. She'd also seen it in the car park of the Royal Hotel.

Something occurred to her. She had asked Skeggsie to find out who the car belonged to. Rose knew that whatever Skeggsie had done to find this out would be illegal – some kind of hacking programme that he had devised, probably into the database at the Driver and Vehicle Licensing Authority.

She opened up the emails that Eddie had sent about the car registration number. He had had to use Skeggsie's computer because Skeggsie had kept the programme he'd devised to himself. She opened Skeggsie's email and clicked on Eddie's file. She read the words in his email.

Once I've input the data I'll leave it to search. I'll take your word for it that it's not traceable (at least not to me!). I trust you.

As soon as Rose asked Skeggsie to find out who owned the car she never saw it in the street again. Not once. Could it be that be the owners of the car somehow *knew* that someone was trying to find out about them? She shook her head. It wasn't possible? Was it? Could it be that the hacking was traced? By the DVLA? Or in some other way?

Had someone monitored Skeggsie's illegal search on his computer? Had someone known what Skeggsie was doing and how?

She sent another email to Eddie.

You'll think this is a stupid question but is it possible for someone's computer activity to be monitored? Like a phone tap but on a computer? How would it be done? Rose

A few moments later she got a reply.

Yep! Absolutely possible. It can be done by cloning. There's software that means that someone can find passwords and replicate what's happening on someone else's computer. It's illegal obviously :-(Will have your picture done in a few mins :-)

The silver SUV stopped watching them just after Skeggsie set up his computer to search for the car's owner. Rose knew that the car was registered to Beaufort Holdings. Why would a company like that want to clone someone's computer? How would they know about Skeggsie or what he was doing? Who would know that Skeggsie had such a lot of hardware? Someone who had been in the flat at some point?

The name James Munroe came into her head. He had been with Skeggsie at the flat in Camden weeks before, waiting for her and Joshua to return so that he could tell them an untrue story about what had happened to their parents.

James Munroe.

Her phone rang. It startled her.

'It's Eddie. I've enlarged your photo.'

'Thanks!'

'Any news on the funeral?'

'Funeral?'

She understood immediately what he meant. Skegg-sie's funeral.

'No, no news. We'll let you know.'

He rang off and Rose sat very still for a second. Had she actually *forgotten* Skeggsie's death amid her excitement and research? After a few moments she blew through her teeth and clicked on Eddie's attachment. The face from the newspaper photograph was clearer if a little blurred.

Was this the woman with the white-blonde hair?

She couldn't be sure.

And yet the face in the picture seemed *familiar* to her. She'd seen it recently.

She'd been looking at photographs in the last couple of days and she was sure she had seen this woman. She stood up feeling excited. She went out of the kitchen and upstairs to the box room. On the floor beside her bed was the photo album that Anna had bought for her. She took it downstairs and placed it by her laptop. She looked at the photo on the screen and then she opened the photo album and turned to the pictures of her mother and her friends. Right at the end she found the photograph she wanted – her mother sitting round a restaurant table with four other women. To her right a dark-haired woman was smiling at the camera.

That woman was Margaret Spicer.

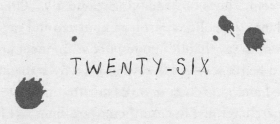

TWENTY-SIX

The front door opened and shut.

'Rose!' Joshua called out.

Rose was sitting in front of the mess of papers on the kitchen table. She was staring at Margaret Spicer's face in the photo alongside her mother. Margaret had the faintest smile on her lips and was holding up a wine glass. The WPC who discovered Judy Greaves's body was a friend of her mother's.

Joshua came into the kitchen and looked quizzically at the things on the table. She closed the photo album and the laptop.

'Sorry I've been out so long but there've been developments.'

He took his coat off and draped it over the back of the chair. She saw him focusing on his uncle's papers and the steel box. She wondered how she was going to explain it all to him.

'I would have rung,' he said, 'but everything was moving quickly. What's going on here?'

'Did you speak to the Polish man?'

'Yeah, but that's not where the developments have come from,' he said, speaking excitedly. 'Greg Tyler walked into the police station an hour ago and gave a new statement to say that he and my uncle *did* meet up on the cliff and had a tussle. He saw him go over the side and panicked and ran. Then it turns out that his wife, Susie, went there later just in case there were signs of life.'

'Oh.'

Rose hadn't expected them to go so soon.

'Joe Warner said they're contradicting each other's stories slightly so there are further interviews to be had. What I can't understand is why Stu hasn't said anything? I can't believe he doesn't remember.'

'Maybe he doesn't want to get Susie into trouble. Maybe he's still hoping she'll come back to him.'

'The woman who left him lying halfway down a cliff?'

Rose shrugged. Joshua continued talking rapidly.

'And if that wasn't enough, Sean Spenser's alibi has collapsed. His mate's mother was out at a club, seen by the barman. Someone did some really good police work there, I have to say. Even Bob was impressed. So the CID are going to talk to him again. I think this might really be it!'

He ran his fingers over the empty steel box.

'What is all this? Why are you looking at it?'

'I had time on my hands . . .' she said, her confidence slipping away in the face of his news.

He shrugged. 'Anyway, I'm going to grab something to eat and I thought we could go over to Bob's. He's in touch with the detectives.'

Rose nodded lamely. The day had been too much for her. The story she had pieced together was overshadowed by Joshua's buoyant mood.

'What did the homeless guy say?'

'Oh God!' Joshua was taking cheese out of the fridge, and bread from the bread bin. 'We had such a runaround at the hospital. It took an age to find out which ward he was in. Then when we got to it he'd been discharged to a hostel. We went there and he was out. We waited and when he came back he was just a little bit tipsy even though he's not supposed to drink while he's at the hostel. So we took him out to a cafe and bought him food and sat with him for about an hour, just chatting generally while he sobered up a bit. Then when I tried talking about Christmas Eve he got confused but eventually he did remember the night. *When it was snowing*, he said. He had the right night in his head.'

'Did he see anyone?'

'No. Well, apart from a woman walking her dog. That was it! We spent most of the day looking for this sad guy and all he could remember was a blonde woman walking her dog.'

A blonde woman walking her dog.

Rose clutched the edge of the table.

'You want some cheese on toast?' Joshua said.

'No.'

'You look upset.'

Rose nodded.

'I'm rambling on here about my day and I keep forgetting that this is all hitting you as well. It's just that this stuff with Sean Spenser is giving me a positive way of dealing with Skeggsie's murder. Something to do instead of sitting around crying. Perhaps you should have come with me today?'

'No, it's not that. I mean I *am* upset about Skeggsie, that goes without saying . . .'

'So what is it?' he said.

'I think I know why he was killed.'

'How do you mean, *why*? I know why he was killed. Rory and Sean . . .'

'No, no. It's to do with this,' she gestured to the things on the table. 'All of this. The Butterfly Murder.'

Joshua gave a half-smile, a look of incredulity.

'Don't be silly.'

'It is. I know it is.'

He put the bread knife down and pushed the bread board away from him. He stood with his back to the work surface and folded his arms across his chest. Rose stuttered the first few words out. It was not going to be easy to explain.

'I think Skeggsie died because of us,' she said. 'You and me and all of this.'

It took a long time to explain. Eventually Joshua sat down, his upper body deflating, his chin resting on the back of his hands. She went through all the things on the table. She didn't refer to the earlier part of her day when she'd talked to Rory and then Susie and Greg Tyler. She focused on Primrose Crescent. She told him about the park and the name of the house and then described her research. She tried to map out what she thought had happened.

'I think that the silver SUV followed us up to Newcastle. You had the number in your book. I checked it. The woman watched us for a few days. Then I asked Skeggsie to find out who it belonged to. He had a way of hacking into databases but his laptop didn't have enough memory so he asked Eddie to go to the flat and set up a search for the number. I think that that search alerted someone to what he was doing. In other words I think his computer has been cloned. Someone has been following what Skeggsie was doing on his computer and that some-one is linked to Beaufort Holdings.'

'But why?'

'Because Beaufort Holdings is linked to the Butterfly Murder. The woman WPC who discovered the girl's body is now a director of the company. The Butterfly Murder involves your uncle and Brendan. And maybe it's the reason for everything that has happened since. Think about it. The significance of the butterfly, the tattoos.'

She rolled her sleeve up, holding her blue butterfly out as if it was evidence.

'I had this done because my mum had one. The same for you with Brendan.'

'And the guy we took the notebooks from had one,' Joshua said.

'If your uncle actually *killed* Simon Lister, as he said in his letter to his solicitor, might Brendan have been involved in some way? And my mum? Maybe on that weekend that they came up to see him in 2004?'

'Wait,' Joshua said. 'Go back to the bit where you said that Skeggsie's computer was cloned. By whom?'

'Whoever did it had to have known that Skeggsie was into computers in a big way. They had to have seen Skeggsie's hardware. They had to have been in the flat.'

'James Munroe.'

Rose sat down and pulled the laptop towards her. She started a new Google search. She put *Beaufort Holdings* in and then *James Munroe*. A magazine article came up. It was from a periodical called *Security Solutions*. She opened it up. It was dated six months before.

Ex-Policemen Make the Best Security Experts.
Ex-Chief Inspector James Munroe gave a talk at the Security Symposium held at Wembley Conference Centre. Munroe celebrated the huge numbers of security consultants who had a background in

policing and he made the point that no one could give better advice than those individuals who had dealt with the criminal classes.

The article went on to describe types of security for gated estates but Rose's eyes were caught by a photo at the bottom of the page. This time it was big enough to tell who the people were.

'Look,' she said, angling the laptop so that Joshua could see the screen.

In the photo James Munroe was standing next to the woman with the white-blonde hair. The caption underneath read, *James Munroe and his wife, Margaret Spicer, Director of Beaufort Holdings.*

'They're *married*!' Rose said with wonder. 'James Munroe married the woman who discovered the body of Judy Greaves. Wait.'

Rose put two more names into the search engine: *James Munroe Simon Lister.* Instantly a long list of items appeared with the names in bold. She picked the first item, dated October 2004.

London Police Chief heads Investigation
Chief Inspector James Munroe from the Metropolitan Police Force has been appointed to oversee the investigation into the handling of enquiries regarding the murder of Simon Lister in August 2004. There

> have been criticisms of the local police force's ability to solve this crime. The local force have been accused of not leading the investigation in a vigorous manner . . .

Joshua opened up a couple of the other references and the articles were similar. He was reading them through and making sounds under his breath, words that Rose couldn't understand. Eventually he stopped reading the screen and slumped back.

'But Skeggsie and I researched James Munroe after Stiffkey, after he told us the lies about Dad and Kathy. We didn't find anything suspicious.'

'Because we didn't know about the Butterfly Murder. We didn't know any of these names until a few days ago. James Munroe is the link in all this . . . Whatever it is. Think about what happened weeks ago. We stumbled on something in Stiffkey and James Munroe and his associates hid it and then told us a pack of lies about Mum and Brendan being dead. James Munroe was there in the flat with Skeggsie when we arrived back from Norfolk.'

'He must have known about the websites we'd set up,' Joshua said thoughtfully. 'Anyone could find those.'

'So he knew that we were searching for them. That's why he told us the story of them being drowned in the car. He wanted to stop us searching.'

'And we did. Skeggsie said for us to keep off the web. Only *talk* about it to each other.'

'Except that he went on a search for the registration number of the SUV.'

'And he got killed for that?'

Rose shrugged. Saying it out loud like that it seemed ridiculous. Who would do such an awful thing? The woman with white-blonde hair?

'They must be hiding something really big. Something so important it's worth an innocent person's life.'

'We need to talk to Margaret Spicer.'

'She was at the Royal Hotel yesterday. I don't know if she's still there.'

'We'll find out,' Joshua said.

They stood up together. Joshua put on the leather bomber jacket. Rose looked around at the table. All these papers had unlocked something for them. She followed Joshua out. The tiredness she had felt had gone. She felt alert. As if something important was going to happen.

TWENTY-SEVEN

The silver SUV was in the car park of the Royal Hotel.

Joshua parked the Mini on the Promenade. The cold weather meant that the parking bays were mostly empty. It was getting dark, the sea was moving lazily back and forth, the sky heavy. The sound of seagulls squawking made Rose look round. Someone had thrown the remains of a bag of chips on to the beach and the birds were in a scrum trying to pluck up the food.

'Where do you think Dad and Kathy stand in all this?' Joshua said.

That was the question, the heart of everything. The hunt for their parents had opened doors to things that they had never wanted to see, experiences they had never wanted to have.

'You think Munroe knows where they are?'

Rose nodded.

'How are we going to handle this?' Joshua said.

'I don't know.'

'If we could get Margaret Spicer out of her room maybe we could go and search it.'

'What are we looking for?' Rose said.

'I don't know. Paperwork? Computer? Anything that might link her and James Munroe to the notebooks?'

'How do we get her out?'

'She was following us, right? So what if I ring her and tell her to come and meet me somewhere that she has to drive to? Say that if she doesn't come I'm going to go to the police. She comes out of the hotel, drives off and if Michelle's on reception I get the key to her room.'

'That's a lot of "ifs".'

'Michelle said she was working nights.'

'What if she won't give you the key?'

'I think she will.'

Joshua made a search on his phone for the number of the hotel. Then he rang it. Rose was tense.

'Good afternoon. Can you put me through to Margaret Spicer's room?'

'Was it Michelle?' Rose whispered.

He shook his head.

He began to speak quietly and firmly to someone on the other end of the line who Rose assumed was Margaret Spicer.

'My name is Joshua Johnson and I believe that you followed me and my friends from London last week.'

There was quiet as Joshua listened.

'My friends saw your car near my house and we also know that you were close to the scene when our friend was killed. I think we need to talk about this now otherwise I will have to go to the police.'

Joshua was listening intently.

'I think your husband, James Munroe, asked you to follow us. I'm wondering whether he also told you to kill my friend, Darren Skeggs, as well.'

Rose held her breath. Joshua's voice was firm.

'Meet me in fifteen minutes' time at the Beacon Shopping Centre in North Shields. You'll know it because of course you are from round here. At least you were when Judy Greaves died.'

A few moments' silence ensued then Joshua ended the call.

'Now we wait,' he said.

'How did she react?'

'She didn't really. She was cool, detached, as if she'd expected me to ring.'

They sat watching the front of the hotel. After a few moments Margaret Spicer came out. For once she didn't have her dog with her. She walked across to her car, pointing the keys at it. The sidelights flashed as it unlocked itself. When she drove off Joshua got out of the car and Rose followed. They walked across the road to the hotel.

Michelle was standing behind the reception desk talking to another member of staff. Her long hair was tied back and she was wearing subtle make-up and tiny gold earrings.

'Hi!' she said brightly, her eyes settling coyly on Joshua's face. 'What can I do for you?'

Joshua looked relieved to see her. He leant on the desk.

'You all right, Michelle? You look nice.'

'Thank you,' she said, looking surprised.

'Would you do something for me . . . For us? I wouldn't ask but it's really important.'

'What?'

Joshua leant across the desk.

'Can you give us the key to Margaret Spicer's room?'

'Why?'

'It's hard to explain. We only need it for ten minutes.'

She turned to Rose. 'This is the woman you asked me about the other day?'

'Yes.'

'Is it to do with Rory or Darren Skeggs?'

Michelle turned round to a row of keys that were hanging up behind her.

'I could lose my job for this.'

'No one will know. When we've opened the door Rose will bring the key back. Then if Margaret Spicer returns you can ring the room. I'll answer and if you don't speak I'll know she's coming back. '

Michelle looked like she was in turmoil.

'This is important, Michelle,' Rose said. 'Please, we wouldn't put you in this position otherwise.'

Michelle turned and picked the key off the wall. She sighed and handed it to Joshua in a theatrical way.

'I owe you one,' he said.

The room was on the second floor. They walked up the stairs and headed along the corridor until they got to Number 213.

Rose was nervous. She looked up and down the hallway to make sure no one else was coming. Then Joshua put the key in the door and turned it. The door opened silently and Rose felt jittery.

'You won't go in until I come back,' she said.

Joshua shook his head.

Rose took the key and dashed back down the corridor. The lift was still there and she stepped into it. She returned the key to Michelle then went back up. Joshua was still standing by the door.

'Ready?' he said.

She nodded. This was something that had to be done.

'Don't turn the light on,' she said. 'If she comes back early she might know someone is in here.'

Joshua walked ahead. The curtains were open and the streetlights shone into the room. It was just possible to see around.

'I'll pull the curtains *then* we can turn on the lights.'

Rose walked past Joshua and headed for the windows.

In between them was a mirror and as she approached it she saw her own shape getting closer. Behind her was Joshua. She looked towards the curtains but her eyes flicked back to the mirror because she thought she noticed some movement. Behind her she heard Joshua make an *Ah!* sound. She spun round and watched him fall to the floor.

'Josh!' she said.

The light went on.

Joshua was face down on the carpet. Behind him, holding a rubber cosh, was James Munroe. He looked flustered. She got down on the floor beside Joshua.

'Are you all right?'

'He'll regain consciousness in a minute,' Munroe said.

She pulled out her mobile and began to push at the buttons but Munroe snatched it from her and tossed it across the room.

'Don't try and ring anyone, Rose, or I'll have to restrain you.'

Joshua began to moan. One hand went up to his head. He rolled round so that he was in a foetal position. James Munroe picked up a pair of cuffs from the bed. He squatted down and took Joshua's other hand and put the cuff on. Then he attached the second cuff to the leg of the bed.

'Shush,' Rose said, lowering her face to Joshua's ear. 'You've been hit on the head but you're all right.'

'Help him to sit up. Lean him against the bed.' Munroe said, his voice sharp, brooking no disagreement.

'You can't stop me walking out of here. Going to the police.'

'I can't stop you. But I thought that you and Joshua wanted to hear the truth. I thought that was what all this childish detective work was about.'

Joshua was half sitting up, pulling at the hand with the cuff on.

'If you pull it the metal will break your skin.'

Rose looked around hopelessly. James Munroe pulled out a chair and sat on it. Behind him was a table and Rose could see a brown suitcase on it. It was exactly like the one that Skeggsie had, where he had put all the stuff that was linked to the notebooks. Munroe saw her looking at it but he didn't comment. On the carpet, by his feet, was a laptop.

'You realise that this meddling of yours only makes your parents' lives more dangerous than they already are?'

At last Munroe was admitting her mother and Brendan were alive. It felt like an important moment.

'Did you kill Darren Skeggs?' Joshua said, struggling to sit up, his cuffed hand at an impossible angle.

'Don't be ridiculous. We do not kill innocent people. What happened to Darren Skeggs was an accident. It was never meant to happen. We sent someone to warn him off, that was all. To tell him to stop his meddling – these searches and websites and hacking programmes. We wanted him to know that we were following his every move and we simply wanted him to stop.'

'So how come he's dead?'

James Munroe looked uncomfortable. He crossed one leg over the other then uncrossed it.

'We asked someone to speak to him, threaten him, if necessary. Not someone in our organisation, you understand. An old contact from the days when Margaret and I worked in the area. This person did what he was told. He spoke to your friend, perhaps roughed him up a little. But your friend put up a fight.'

Rose stared at the man. *He spoke to your friend, perhaps roughed him up a little.* It was a euphemism for saying that some thug pulled Skeggsie into the alley and gave him a beating while at the same time demanding that he stop the search for their parents.

'Not exactly an equal match – your *associate* with a knife and Skeggsie using his fists,' Joshua said.

'Well, Joshua, you should ask yourself who exactly put this young man in danger. If you hadn't involved him he might still be alive.'

Was he saying that it was *Joshua's fault* that Skeggsie was killed?

Joshua pulled at the cuff on his arm and tried to kick his legs out in the direction of James Munroe. Munroe flinched.

'What happened to Skeggsie?' Rose insisted.

'Your friend fought back. He was ferocious we were told. Our associate was cornered. He hadn't expected any trouble. He said he had no choice.'

Tears sprang into Rose's eyes.

Why did you put up a fight? she thought. *Why this time?*

But she knew the answer. Skeggsie had been fired up after the drama in the pub smoking area. He'd wanted to stand his ground. Possibly he'd thought that by standing up to this person he was making a stand against all the bullies he'd ever faced, even making a stand against Joshua's protectiveness. Instead of accepting a couple of punches and threats he had put up a proper fight for the first time in his life.

'We are sorry. Our organisation never meant for this to happen but the boy was digging into things he couldn't possibly understand and maybe, in the long run, putting our operatives' lives at risk, including those of your parents. I can't say any more about it than that.'

Rose didn't speak. James Munroe was looking less formal than she'd ever seen him, wearing a jumper over a T-shirt. His shoes had been heavily polished, neat brown leather lace-ups. The upset hadn't affected his sense of wardrobe.

'He's dead because he looked up a car registration number?' Joshua said, his voice breaking.

'No. If we'd wanted to hide Margaret's identity we would have changed the plates on her car. No, Margaret runs a respectable security company. I am a civil servant. We have nothing to hide.'

'Why then?' Rose said.

'Because of all this.' James Munroe swivelled round to the brown suitcase and flipped up the lid. 'All this meddling. It seems that your young friend spent hours and hours trying to decode these books which should never have existed in the first place. Unfortunately one of our organisation took it into his head to document every mission that we carried out.'

He took out one of the notebooks by the corner as if it was something disgusting that he couldn't bear to hold. Rose thought of Frank Richards, the man with the suitcase on wheels. He'd been the first person to tell them that their parents were alive. Joshua had stolen the notebooks from him and Skeggsie had revelled in trying to decipher the code. It had taken him weeks to decode a couple of pages.

'You stole Skeggsie's suitcase?'

'We are security specialists. It's not hard for us to enter a property.'

'You stabbed him?' Joshua said.

Munroe shook his head. 'We are a professional organisation, Joshua. We're not criminals. But perhaps we should get down to the real point of this meeting.'

'What is the point of this meeting?'

'It's time for your parents to speak to you. Maybe you will listen to them.'

Rose sat up with start. Joshua looked around warily.

'Maybe you will finally understand how important our work is.'

Rose stared at the door, expecting it to open.

Was this the moment that they would see their parents again?

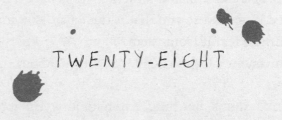

TWENTY-EIGHT

James Munroe leant down to the carpet and picked up a laptop. He opened it and sat it on his lap. Rose felt her hopes dashed in a second. There was going to be no physical meeting after all. Just some communication from them, an email perhaps, some words that Munroe would claim that they had written. It would be like what happened weeks ago when he took them to Childerley Waters and showed them a picture of a car that had been pulled from the reservoir weeks before. Their parents' bodies had sat in that car for five years, he'd lied.

Now he was going to try something similar.

She would not believe a word of it.

Joshua was staring dully at Munroe as though the same thoughts were going through his head.

'Your parents have asked me to pass this on to you,' Munroe said.

Rose crossed her arms and stared at the carpet.

'They are in great danger . . .'

'From Lev Baranski?' Joshua said.

'From various sources. They are in hiding. They are working on a mission and if their cover is blown they will be killed. I can assure you that *is* the truth. But don't take it from me. Hear it from them.'

'A mission?' Joshua said. 'So it is about national security?'

Munroe shook his head emphatically. He tapped on some keys and then turned the laptop round so that it was facing them. Rose moved forward but Joshua could not. How was he supposed to read the email?

After a couple of seconds a still picture appeared.

It was an image of Brendan and her mother.

Rose gasped. Joshua grabbed her arm with his free hand.

Rose got closer still. It was a head and shoulders shot. Brendan was in front, closest to the camera, his head bigger; her mother was behind him, only two-thirds of her face showing. Brendan was clean-shaven with no hair and he was wearing pebble-shaped glasses. He looked thinner but Rose would still have recognised him. Her mother's hair was pulled back and she was wearing heavy framed black glasses. She was pale and seemed to be clenching her jaw.

Munroe pressed a couple of buttons and the still image started to move. Brendan's face had a puzzled look on it, her mother was staring intently at the screen.

'Is it working?' her mother said.

'I think so, here . . .' Brendan said, his fingers coming up to the screen.

It made Rose's heart soar to see them.

'Rose and Joshua, I know you're watching this and I know that both of you must be angry about what has happened but I wanted – *we* wanted – you to know that what we have done is for the greater good.'

He paused as if he was thinking before he went ahead. Her mother seemed to say something in his ear.

'Kathy wants you to know how much she loves you, Rose, and of course, Josh, the same goes for me.'

Rose felt her hand go out to the screen as if she might touch it.

'Rose,' Brendan said, coughing, his hand over his mouth. 'You spoke to me a couple of hours ago on Stu's phone. I had no idea about his accident. I was there with him on the cliff but he was OK when I left. I don't know what to say . . . And Josh, I believe you tried to contact us on the same number . . .'

A couple of hours ago? Rose spoke to Brendan on Christmas Eve, almost a week ago. Her mother's face came more into view. She looked tense and unhappy. It was a Skype recording and the quality wasn't good. It was jerky and looked as though it might disintegrate at any moment.

Brendan carried on speaking.

'Josh and Rose, I'm going to try and explain to you why we are doing what we are doing. Then you have to back off. It's dangerous for you to get anywhere near us. There are people who are looking for us and if they think you know anything then your lives are in danger.'

Kathy edged closer to the camera. 'Rose, this is why we left. This is why we had to go.'

Rose's mouth went dry. Her mother's hand was out as if she might reach through the screen to touch her.

'I'll start at the beginning. In 2004 just after Kathy and I got together I visited Stuart in Newcastle. I took Kathy with me. Stuart was very wound up about one of his students whose sister had been murdered two years before. The man had got away with it. Stuart had become obsessed about it. While we were up there he got very drunk and showed me where the man lived. He also showed me a knife he'd put aside in order to kill this man. I tried to placate him and promised him my team would help with the investigation. I was really worried about him. He seemed unhinged. I thought he had calmed down but that night he stormed out and came back later covered in blood. I couldn't believe that he'd done such a thing and he told me that he'd dropped the knife in the man's garden. The killing was premeditated. I knew he would spend a lifetime in prison for it and I couldn't let that happen. I went round to the garden where the dead man was and I combed the crime scene. I found the knife and I disposed of it. He was my brother, I had to help him out. In the days that followed the police found evidence of this man's intention to kill another girl and they also found belongings of other missing girls. Stuart was ecstatic. It wasn't a murder, he said, it was punishment. It was an execution.'

Brendan stopped.

'What the police found in Simon Lister's house would have shocked the most experienced officers. Some of it came out in the papers. Kathy and I were back in London but because we were serving officers it was easy for us to find out the facts. This made us think about the things we were doing, the cases we were involved in.'

Rose's attention was on her mother's face. Her eyes seemed hollowed out behind her glasses. She looked tired and older, as if more than twice five years had passed since Rose last saw her.

'Many of us, people like James Munroe and Frank Richards, we were all fed up with criminals literally getting away with murder. We worked on cold cases. We saw it every day. Men who had been responsible for murder and drug dealing, trafficking and prostitution. But these weren't the men who went to prison or who were even arrested. They sat in plush homes and lived off the earnings of legions of small-time crooks. So we decided to do something about it. We decided to mete out justice. And when people were guilty of murder, people like Viktor Baranski, we punished them.'

'No . . .' Joshua said.

'I can't say any more because the less you know the better. I've told you this now to stop you looking into it any more. I also want you never to mention this to your uncle. When he comes out of hospital you have to put it out of your mind. It was a moment of madness for him. He's not been involved since and he wouldn't hurt a fly.'

Brendan seemed to turn away for a moment and mumbled something to her mother. Rose was frowning. She thought about what Stuart had said to Greg Tyler on the cliff walk. *The world would be a better place if you were out of it.* She hadn't told this to Joshua. Had Stuart really *intended* to hurt Greg Tyler?

'In a few months Kathy and I will have done our last job. Then we will contact you.'

The screen went black suddenly but not before Rose saw her mother's mouth open as if she had something to say. Rose sat up straight, disconcerted.

'That can't be all there is?' she said.

James Munroe had turned the laptop round so that the screen was facing him. He began hitting the keys.

'Wait!' she said, standing up, stepping towards him, grabbing hold of the corner of the laptop. 'There must be more. Wait. I want to see it again!'

'Deleted!'

'No,' Rose said. 'I just want to look at it again.'

'That was the agreement we had with your father and

your mother. You could see it once and then it had to be deleted.'

'You had no right . . .'

Rose felt herself heating up.

'It was Brendan's wish. You heard what he said.'

Munroe was closing the laptop, his hands gently pulling it down until it clicked.

'NO! YOU HAD NO RIGHT. THAT WAS MY MOTHER!'

Munroe stood up. He towered over Rose. His face had no expression. He'd deleted her mother. He'd pressed a button and erased the faces and the words and the life that had been on that screen. She'd hardly spoken, just stayed at Brendan's shoulder, backing him up with her presence. And yet it had seemed in some way as if she had spent the time staring into the camera as though she'd been peering through a window at Rose, the daughter she hadn't seen for five years.

She looked round at Joshua, still handcuffed to the leg of the bed. He was staring at the carpet, suppressed fury on his face. Munroe had deleted Brendan as well.

After a moment of bright light they were back in the dark.

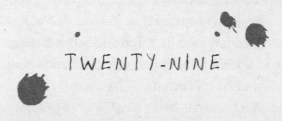

TWENTY-NINE

Moments later Margaret Spicer came into the room.

Close up she looked thinner, the veins on her neck sticking out. Rose studied her face to see the resemblance between her now and in the photo with her mum in the restaurant. She couldn't tell because Margaret Spicer wouldn't make eye contact.

'Where's the dog?' she said.

She surveyed the room, her eyes skimming across Rose, who was sitting on the floor next to Joshua.

'In the bathroom.'

'Are the cuffs absolutely necessary?'

'I think so.'

'Have they seen the Skype?'

'They have. Which is probably why they're both so quiet.'

Margaret Spicer looked ill at ease. Rose pictured her on Christmas Eve, walking past the alley while someone was in there waiting for Skeggsie. Maybe Skeggsie passed her and she said to him something like *Was that a noise there? Is someone hurt?* in the same way that she, Rose, had said it to Joshua. Skeggsie would have gone straight to see who was there. He wouldn't have linked this woman to the car that had been following them. In any case he wouldn't have thought for a second that his life was in any danger. Perhaps it had happened differently. Margaret Spicer may have been walking *after* Skeggsie and may have signalled to the associate who was waiting to warn him off. If only they'd known Skeggsie a little bit. They might have understood then that they could never have warned him off.

The woman was an unlikely assassin and yet she had been the intermediary. She was as guilty as James Munroe.

'Now we go?' Margaret Spicer said to Munroe.

Munroe nodded.

'Don't you care?' Rose said. 'Don't you *care* that our friend is dead?'

Margaret Spicer looked startled at being spoken to.

Munroe spoke. 'Margaret was patrolling Primrose Crescent when a young male estate agent ran out of a house screaming. He was hysterical and Margaret tried to calm him down. He kept pulling her arm and in the end she followed him into Number Six. She saw Judy Greaves's body. Five days the girl was missing. When she found her the girl was still *warm*. Lister had her for five days. He killed her an hour or so before he'd arranged to meet the estate agent in the house. The estate agent was hysterical but Margaret sat with the girl until the authorities came. Margaret knows how important this project is. She doesn't want to see guilty people get away.'

'Can't she speak for herself?'

The woman was holding clothes that she'd taken out of a drawer. Rose noticed then an open suitcase on the floor. They were leaving. It seemed as though as soon as she and Joshua sniffed these people out they packed a suitcase and left.

'You found Judy. We found Skeggsie. How does that make you feel?'

'This is about the bigger picture, Rose,' Munroe said. 'It was a mistake and we must move on.'

Margaret Spicer continued to pack. Munroe stared at Joshua uneasily.

'The Skype recording was made on Christmas Eve, right?' Joshua said. 'A few hours after Rose spoke to my dad when he rang my uncle. Midday.'

Munroe nodded.

'So my dad knows nothing about Skeggsie's murder.'

'What makes you think that? There are no secrets in our organisation.'

'My dad couldn't have spoken to me like that if he'd known that my best friend was dead, killed by you. He couldn't have looked me in the eye with that knowledge in his head.'

Rose thought of Brendan looking Joshua in the eye. In reality it had been the tiny lens of a camera embedded into the screen of a laptop. Had Brendan seen through that? Had he, in his mind, looked into the eyes of the son he hadn't seen for so long?

'Your father has gone through a lot. He's not the same man you knew.'

'He's still my dad. He would never hurt me knowingly. He didn't know about Skeggsie's murder, did he?'

'We should go,' Margaret Spicer said.

James Munroe stood up, placing the laptop in its carrying case. He stacked it next to the case that they were packing on the floor. Then he picked up the brown suitcase. Rose looked at it with concern. It was Skeggsie's and full of the things that he'd thought were important about the Murder Notebooks. It held the very things that had got him killed. Now Munroe had it.

'You haven't told him. My dad's not any part of Skeggsie's murder.'

'I don't call it a murder. I call it an accident.'

'What makes you think we're not going to go straight to the police as soon as you've gone?' Joshua said.

'You can of course. But I tell you this, Joshua. If the police come for me or Margaret I will reveal everything that has happened in the last five years and your father and your mother will be exposed. And don't for a minute think that I mean they will be *arrested*. No, no. They have upset a number of people and if I expose their whereabouts then they will most certainly endure a horrible death.'

'Come on,' Margaret Spicer said. 'Let's go.'

'In the last five years six evil men have been removed from our society. That is a good thing. I'm very sorry about your friend.'

He stood at the door. In moments they would be gone.

'What about Joshua?' Rose said, pointing to the cuff attached to the leg of the bed.

'I fear if I free Joshua now he will make some dramatic stand and there will be unpleasantness. Rose, you come down to the car with us. As we're about to leave I will give you the key to the handcuffs.'

Unpleasantness. Such a polite word. Did Munroe think that Skeggsie's murder was *unpleasant,* she wondered.

Margaret Spicer was walking round the room, opening drawers. Then she opened the bathroom door. The small dog walked out, wagging its tail. It hadn't made a sound the whole time they'd been there. Perhaps it was well trained. Margaret hooked a lead on to its neck, picked up a bag, and went out without a backwards glance.

James Munroe followed her with the rest of the bags.

'I'll be back as soon as I can,' Rose said to Joshua, going out of the door.

Rose stood by the silver SUV as Margaret Spicer put her case on to the back seat of the car. In the passenger seat the dog stood on his hind legs and looked out of the window. Its tail was wagging and its eyes were following Margaret as she walked round to the driver's seat and got into the car.

Munroe put his laptop on top of Skeggsie's brown suitcase.

'Why do you have to take that stuff? It's important to us.'

'This is what got you into trouble. Forget about all this. Your parents will contact you when they are ready. Here are the keys to the handcuffs. Goodbye, Rose.'

She stood and watched as the car swung out of the car park and on to the Promenade. When it was gone she turned and quickly went back into the hotel. Michelle looked up from the reception desk but Rose waved her question away and rushed past. When she got back to Room 213 Joshua moved impatiently around, holding out his hand for her to undo the lock on the cuffs. She squatted down as quickly as she could and undid the lock. The cuff fell apart and Joshua held his wrist. There was a red ring where the skin had rubbed. As soon as he was free he stood up, his fists clenched and walked to the window. If he was looking for the SUV it was long gone.

'Where's my phone?' he said.

It was over by the bathroom door. She picked it up and held it out to him. He didn't take it, though. His back was to her and he was staring out of the window. She stayed away from him. His anger had been boiling up while he'd been stuck in one place and she didn't want to be near him if it erupted now. She looked at the screen of his phone. He had a new message. She didn't know whether to tell him or not.

Her mother's face came back into her head, the black glasses were new, the frames heavier than she usually wore. Perhaps that was part of her disguise. Brendan said they were on their last mission. It meant that they were planning to kill some gangster, someone who deserved to die. Would her mother actually take part in that act?

Joshua was looking at her. His haggard expression seemed to reflect everything they'd learned and heard over the last hours. They were bewildered. Abandoned children who thought they'd lost everything five years ago. How little they'd known then.

Then he was beside her. He took his phone and then hooked his other arm around her neck and pulled her towards him. She felt as if he was overheating, the back of his jumper damp. She rubbed her face against the wool and put her arms around him. He was staring at his phone.

'Look at this,' he said, his voice soft in her ear.

She looked at the screen of his phone. There was a message. **We only just found out about your friend's death. We're more sorry than we can say. We would never have let this happen but some things seem to have got out of hand. We love you both and talk about**

you every day. One day we will be together again. XXXX
Dad (and Mum).

'They didn't know,' Joshua said, the thinnest of smiles on his lips. 'They knew nothing about Skeggsie's death.'

Rose nodded staring at the word *Mum*. In brackets.

'I was right. Dad and Kathy were innocent of that,' Joshua said.

But guilty of other things, Rose thought. *Guilty of murder.*

THIRTY

The house was straight by the time Stuart Johnson came out of hospital. Everything had been cleaned and tidied. The pay as you go mobile phone had been placed back into the small money box, locked and put among Stuart's things from his school locker. The other steel box had been refilled with all the paperwork from the Butterfly Murder, locked and wrapped in a tea towel. They then placed it in the engine of the MG. Joshua fastened the spare wheel in place again and then they covered the old car with tarpaulin and locked the garage door.

Joshua replaced Stuart's confession in the envelope and glued the opening together. Then he put it back into the Last Will and Testament package and put it in his bedside cabinet drawer.

Everything was as it had been before they'd arrived there.

Now Stuart would have no idea that his secret had been discovered.

He was smiling as he got out of the taxi and looked up at the house with some relief. No doubt, during that long night on the ledge of the cliff, he may have thought he would never see it again. Rose felt an unexpected wash of pity for him. He didn't look like Brendan at all. He was younger and shorter and his skin was florid. He leant on Joshua as he came up the path. Joshua's face was unreadable. At one point he gave a little laugh and Rose wondered how he could pretend.

Just for a day, Rosie. Just pretend none of it ever happened just for a day. Then we'll get off back to London, Joshua had said.

Part of Stuart's leg was in a cast and he was still a bit bruised and ill-looking. He moved awkwardly along the hallway and then into the living room and sat down with a thump on a chair. Rose stayed with him while Joshua made some drinks. He grabbed her hand and held it tightly and told her how sorry he was about her friend. She kept a smile on her face and asked him about his injuries. Then they talked about the hospital and how long it would be before he got back to work.

Joshua brought the bomber jacket and gave it to him. Stuart liked it, Rose could tell. He was smiling and looked it over, remarking on all the pocket space and well worn leather. He said he couldn't wait to wear it.

They kept the pretence up.

Nothing difficult was mentioned.

In the afternoon there was a knock on the door and when Rose opened it Susie Tyler was standing there. Beside her was a large holdall. Rose brought her in and she rushed into the living room and sat down by Stuart and hugged him. Her ponytail bobbed up and down as she burst into tears and said how glad she was that he was alive and how much she loved him.

She'd been seeing him in the hospital for a few days and told him that she'd left Greg for good and was coming to live with him so that they could have their baby together. Joshua and Rose had looked with disbelief at the pair.

She left him to die, Rose thought as Susie rushed upstairs to unpack her bag. But Stuart was beaming and humming tunes all evening.

The next day the Mini sat under the shadow of the Angel of the North. It was New Year's Day and the sun was a dazzling globe hanging in a flat blue sky. The Angel's wings threw a shaft of darkness across the fields and the car park. Rose cricked her neck to look out of the car window to see the very top, the faceless creature that she'd seen in the poster in Skeggsie's bedroom.

They were on their way back to London.

Everything was packed into the back of the Mini.

Joshua was looking at his mobile phone. Rose wondered if they were going to get out or sit there. She didn't ask

– she just let the silence hang in the air. This was how things had worked over the last few days. They were together and yet there was this great unspoken mass of stuff between them.

There were groups of people making their way across the fields and from the road towards the great statue. In the distance she could see a train going past. No doubt there were people there looking out of the window, pointing at this monolith. Skeggsie had wanted to take Joshua to see it. Rose imagined the two of them looking up at the metal giant, Skeggsie giving Joshua as much information as he had. *Wings the width of those of a jumbo jet!* Maybe Joshua would talk about the engineering aspect of the statue, how many men it had taken to make it, the erection of it, the welding. *Not so different from a bridge*, she imagined Skeggsie saying, just to please Joshua.

She felt her throat go hard and tried to swallow a couple of times. She was near to tears so she turned and looked in the other direction towards Newcastle. It was the place where Skeggsie was brought up and now would never leave.

Joshua was staring out of the window towards the Angel. He didn't look as if he was going to say anything. She closed her eyes and laid her head on the headrest.

She was tired.

The investigation into Skeggsie's death was continuing. Bob Skeggs had come round to see them a couple of evenings before. There had been some good news on the forensic front. Skeggsie had put up a fight. They had found skin and blood under his fingernails. It meant they had a DNA sample and although it hadn't matched anything at the moment it would be on the database. On top of that some shop CCTV cameras further along Jesmond Road had picked up an image of a young man in a balaclava walking away from the scene round about eleven twenty. They'd also picked up an image of a woman with light-coloured hair walking her dog but Bob Skeggs had laughed this off. *It was one of those Jack Russell dogs*, he'd said.

It was too soon to talk about a funeral for Skeggsie, Bob had said, but as soon as it was set he would let them know. Bob had insisted again that Joshua use Skeggsie's car and the flat until the end of the academic year. Then they would think again. When Bob got up to leave Joshua followed him out into the hall and she heard them talking for what seemed like a long while. When he came back in he looked tearful and turned the television on, the sound loud.

They'd talked about their parents and the Butterfly Murder but only ever for a short while. The conversation started well but quickly drifted into acrimony. Joshua had become defensive and said that they hadn't heard the whole story, that they didn't know all the facts. Rose sank into gloom. They knew one fact for sure. Their parents were involved in murder, assassination, whatever name they wanted to give it. It was not something that Rose could stomach.

There was a beep in the car.

'New message,' Joshua said, his voice breaking the quiet.

She looked over to see who the message was from. The name Bob Skeggs was there.

'Why is Skeggsie's dad texting you?'

'I asked him to do something for me.'

'What?'

'I asked him to pull some strings and trace the origin of the text message I got from Dad and Kathy.'

Rose didn't say anything. She stared at her hands.

'It's a difficult thing to do. It needs all sorts of warrants but Bob's in a good position at the moment. A lot of people are feeling sorry for him and he can ask a few favours. So he asked someone he knows in the Drugs Squad to do it and they did.'

She wasn't going to speak. She wasn't going to be drawn into this any more. She was leaving the past behind. Joshua didn't notice her silence and went on talking.

'They can only triangulate an area that it might have come from. Here, he's given me some postcodes . . .'

Joshua got Google Maps on his phone.

'Look, somewhere between Wickby, Southwood and Hensham. That's where the text came from.'

'Why have you done this?'

'I want to know where they are, Rose.'

Rose looked at the triangle on the map. Three small villages in Essex.

'Dad sent the text from there. Doesn't mean that's where they are but that text was sent in a hurry. I'm guessing they're somewhere in that area.'

'Doing what? Waiting to kill someone?'

'I don't know. But whatever they're doing I'm going to find them. I'm not going to give up. I have to go on. For Skeggsie's sake.'

Joshua's hand was on hers. She knew she would support him whatever he wanted to do but in her heart she didn't want to get involved. Not now that she knew the truth.

'Come on,' he whispered. 'let's go and see the Angel, close up. The way Skeggsie wanted.'

They got out of the car and walked towards the Angel, its arms out as if welcoming them.

THE MURDER NOTEBOOKS

Your parents are dead – or so everyone says.
How much would you risk to find out the truth

  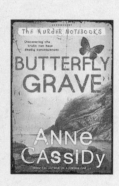

OUT NOW

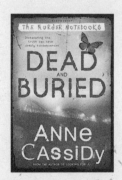

COMING SOON